6
SUGAR CREEK GANG
The SECRET HIDEOUT

Paul Hutchens

MOODY PUBLISHERS
CHICAGO

Original Title: *Sugar Creek Gang in School*

ISBN-10: 0-8024-7010-6
ISBN-13: 978-0-8024-7010-2

We hope you enjoy this book from Moody Publishers.
Our goal is to provide high-quality, thought-provoking
books and products that connect truth to your real needs
and challenges. For more information on other books
and products written and produced from a biblical per-
spective, go to www.moodypublishers.com or write to:

Moody Publishers
820 N. LaSalle Boulevard
Chicago, IL 60610

10

PREFACE

Hi—from a member of the Sugar Creek Gang!

It's just that I don't know which one I am. When I was good, I was Little Jim. When I did bad things—well, sometimes I was Bill Collins or even mischievous Poetry.

You see, I am the daughter of Paul Hutchens, and I spent many an hour listening to him read his manuscript as far as he had written it that particular day. I went along to the north woods of Minnesota, to Colorado, and to the various other places he would go to find something different for the Gang to do.

Now the years have passed—more than fifty, actually. My father is in heaven, but the Gang goes on. All thirty-six books are still in print and now are being updated for today's readers with input from my five children, who also span the decades from the '50s to the '70s.

The real Sugar Creek is in Indiana, and my father and his six brothers were the original Gang. But the idea of the books and their ministry were and are the Lord's. It is He who keeps the Gang going.

PAULINE HUTCHENS WILSON

1

If I hadn't been the janitor of our little one-room red brick schoolhouse, I don't suppose I would have cared so much when Poetry's wet pet lamb walked around all over the floor with his muddy feet.

Lambs, you know, are not supposed to go to school, and even though the Sugar Creek Gang knew that, they thought they'd like to see what it was like to have one come in spite of the fact that it was, as a certain poem says, "against the rule."

It certainly made the children laugh and play—and it also made some of them cry and work, especially me. That is, I had to mop the floor, and I had to stay in at recess to do it, with Poetry and all the rest of the gang helping me. It took longer to get the floor clean than it should have, because the lamb accidentally turned over a pail of sudsy water, and it scattered itself in every direction there was.

Maybe before I tell you what the teacher said about the lamb at school, I'd better explain why it was there, and who I mean when I say "Poetry," and also when I say "The Sugar Creek Gang," because maybe you've never heard about us. Then you'll understand that we really weren't trying to get ourselves into trouble when we took that innocent lamb to school that Monday morning.

The idea had first come to us when we were having our gang meeting the second Saturday after school started. We held our meeting in an abandoned graveyard away up on the other side of Bumblebee Hill, which is the nickname for Strawberry Hill that we'd given it after we'd killed a bear and later fought a tough town gang there. In fact, the bumblebees helped us lick that tough, swearing bunch of boys.

As I said, the second Saturday after school started, we had our gang meeting in that spooky old cemetery, which they didn't bury people in anymore. And that was the time we decided to let Poetry's lamb follow him to school the very next Monday morning.

Right after dinner that Saturday, after I'd dried the dishes and Mom and Dad had both said I didn't have to work that afternoon, I made a dive for our kitchen door. I stopped outside only long enough to keep the door from slamming, so it wouldn't wake up my little one-year-old baby sister, Charlotte Ann. Then like a wild deer, I galloped out across our grassy yard, passed the big walnut tree with the high swing in it, swished across the road past our tin mailbox, which had on it *Theodore Collins,* my Dad's name. And then I touched one hand on the top rail of the fence, vaulted over, and ran.

Ran, I tell you, straight down the path through the woods that leads to the spring. At the biggest tree I swerved to the right and followed another path, which had been made by boys' feet. Soon, gasping and panting and swinging my straw hat, I was at the bottom of Bumblebee Hill, where the gang was supposed to meet first.

We all had a spooky feeling about meeting in that graveyard because there were so many stories in the world about graveyards having ghosts in them. So we'd planned to all go there together, and if there *were* any ghosts, we could —well, we could all run away together anyway.

I'd stopped to get rid of some of my extra breath, always having too much after running like that, when I heard a noise of underbrush crashing and breaking and a heavy body running.

I looked up, and there lumbering toward me was my best friend, Leslie Thompson, whose nickname is Poetry. Right that same minute he saw me, and he began to quote between puffs one of his more than one hundred memorized poems. It was about the wind, which I guess his heavy breathing had reminded him of. It went like this:

> I saw you toss the kites on high
> And blow the birds about the sky;
> And all around I heard you pass
> Like ladies' skirts across the grass—
> O wind, a-blowing all day long!
> O wind, that sings so loud a song!

That was one of my favorite poems.

Pretty soon Poetry and I were lying in the long mashed-down grass, watching the white clouds hanging in the lazy blue sky and listening to each other catch his breath.

He started quoting the second verse, getting about halfway through when he was very suddenly interrupted by somebody's spraying water in his face with a squirt gun.

Even I was half mad for a minute, because some of the water spattered in *my* face. Besides, I'd been sort of dreaming about the wind that Poetry's poem was describing, and nobody likes to have his thoughts interrupted.

Poetry had just been saying:

"I saw the different things you did,
But always, you, yourself, you hid;
I felt you push, I heard you call,
I could not see yourself at all . . ."

Then he started to gasp and sputter and get red in the face and roll over and sit up and say something, and from the bushes behind us there came a squawky voice, imitating Poetry's. It said:

"The rain is raining all around,
It rains on field and tree;
It rains on umbrellas here,
And on the ships at sea."

I knew right away which one of the Sugar Creek Gang it was, because he was the only one of us who was more disgusted than the rest of us with Poetry's poetry. He was always quoting one of them himself just to make it seem ridiculous. Even if I hadn't heard his voice and seen his brown hair on his hatless head, his blue eyes, and monkeylike face, I'd have known it was Circus.

He came cartwheeling toward us in grand style, just like an acrobat on a county fair stage, only better.

The next minute Circus and Poetry and I were all in a tangled-up scramble like a bunch of boys in a football game. Poetry especially was grunting and trying to unroll himself from the rest of us. In fact, our six pairs of legs and arms, making twelve altogether, sort of looked like a lot of fishing worms in a knot.

We hadn't any more than unscrambled ourselves when there came more running feet in our direction, and in another minute we were four instead of three. This time it was a spindle-legged little guy with very large, bulging eyes and a nose that was crooked at the end. His actual name was Roy Gilbert, but we called him Dragonfly, because his eyes were enormous—almost too big for his little head, which a *real* dragonfly's eyes are, but which, of course, Dragonfly's eyes weren't.

That little chattering, pop-eyed member of our gang was always seeing things before the rest of us were, and sometimes he saw things that really weren't there at all. He was right though, when he saw that big savage bear, which we killed and which I told you about in one of the other Sugar Creek Gang stories. He was also right the time he saw that bank robber, whom we helped capture. On top of that, Dragonfly was also right when he saw the ghost running— or flying or something—in that same old cemetery one night.

But that's almost telling you a secret that I'm saving until another chapter and which didn't happen until after Poetry's innocent lamb had followed him to school.

Anyway, pretty soon Big Jim, the leader of our gang, came swishing down the path. He stopped in the shade of the bushes beside us and started catching his breath like the rest of us. I couldn't help but notice that the little fuzzy mustache he had shaved off just before we had taken our trip to Chicago was still off, with not even a sign of its having begun to grow again. In fact, it hadn't been long enough to shave in the first place. Big Jim was a great leader, I tell you—a fierce fighter and as strong as anything. His hands were calloused from hard work, which he even *liked* to do.

Each one of us lay in a different direction, chattering away and waiting for the rest to come.

Little Jim, our smallest, was nearly always late because he had to practice his piano lesson right after the noon meal each Saturday. He was getting to be a great player, his mom being the best musician in all Sugar Creek territory.

Pretty soon I heard somebody coming. I looked around a corner of the elder bush I was lying under, and it was Little Jim, just poking along, barefoot, his new, clean blue denim overalls rolled up halfway to his knees and his half-worn-out brown straw hat on backward and his little mouselike face looking very content. He was carrying an ash stick about three feet long, with stripes on it, the stripes having been made with his pocketknife by cutting off the bark, so that it looked like a big three-foot-long piece of stick candy.

"Hi, Little Jim!" different ones of us called to him.

He kept on doing what he was doing, which was knocking off the tops of different weeds with his stick, not paying any attention to us. Then he stooped and rolled up his right overall leg, which had just come down. While he was still stooped over, he grunted, "Hi, everybody." Then he straightened up and grinned.

Little Jim flopped himself down beside us just in time to get up with us, for at that same minute from the other direction came little red-haired, freckled-faced Tom Till, the new member of our gang. Fiery-tempered Tom was a great guy even if his big brother, Bob, had caused us, especially Big Jim, a lot of trouble.

Anyway, the minute Little Jim and Tom got there, we scrambled to our different-sized bare feet and started up Bumblebee Hill to the cemetery and—you can believe this or not—to run into another mystery, which I'll tell you about as soon as I get to it.

Writing a story, you know, is like building a

tall building. If you put the top on first, without any good foundation, the house will fall down. So I have to save the top of the story, which is the mystery, for later. And the mystery is the ghost that Dragonfly saw one very dark night.

"Here we go," Big Jim called to us, unfolding his long legs and rambling up the hill with the rest of us scurrying after him. Suddenly he stopped, looked back at us, and with a strange expression on his mustacheless face said, "Anybody afraid?"

And we yelled a big noisy "No!"—all except Dragonfly, whose mother was what is called a superstitious person and actually believed in such things as ghosts. She even believed that if a black cat ran across the road in front of you, it meant you were going to have bad luck.

Anyway, when Dragonfly didn't act as though he was glad we were going up to have our meeting in the old cemetery, I knew the reason, and I felt sorry for him.

"Come on, fraidy-cat!" I said and grabbed him by the arm.

Poetry grabbed him by the other arm, and away we went to make plans that were going to make some of the schoolchildren laugh and play and some of them cry and work.

We certainly didn't know, when we started up that hill for our first fall gang meeting, that the whole fall was going to be filled with exciting adventures. One especially was going to make my fiery red hair stand on end and scare me and the rest of the gang half to death.

2

Poetry was puffing along beside me. Seeing what I had in my hand, he said, "Our new teacher wants us to gather all kinds of weed seeds and classify them."

He took the long, green, empty flower spike out of my hand and looked at it like a college professor and said in a deep, important-sounding voice, "*That*, Bill Collins, is blue vervain. In the middle of summer, here at the bottom, there was a little blue flower ring, which, as summer moved along, slowly crept up the spike, the old flowers dying and the new ones coming out, until finally the ring slipped off the nice green lady's finger—I mean, it slipped off Lucille's finger."

Bang! Something inside me fired up when he said that, and that was the end of *that* speech. The next thing Poetry knew, he was lying flat on the grass beside a wild rosebush where I'd shoved him, sticking out my foot to trip him at the same time.

"I don't *like* her!" I yelled down at him, meaning I didn't want anybody to know that I thought Circus's ordinary-looking sister, whose name was Lucille, had nice curls.

You see, ever since last year, when I'd tried to kill a spider for one of Circus's many sisters, some of the gang—Poetry especially—had been teasing me about her. And I wouldn't stand for it. In fact, if there's anybody I like less than anybody else, it's some awkward *girl*, although Circus's sister did have nice curls.

Big Jim led us into the middle of the old graveyard to where there was a big pine tree, and right beside it on the west side stood a tall tombstone with a square base. The rest of it was shaped like a monument in a city park. The grass there was nice and long, so we all dropped down, half sitting and half lying, each one of us chewing grass stems, like cows when they rest and chew their cuds. And there we had our meeting.

And then, while I was lying on my back with my elbows up and my hands folded under the back of my head, I saw on the tall monument-shaped tombstone something that made me sit up and gasp. I had the funniest feeling when I realized what I was seeing.

"'S'matter?" Dragonfly wanted to know, looking scared and not feeling very good about having the meeting there anyway.

"Look at that, will you?" I sort of half whispered and pointed to what was above the name on the tombstone. In fact, I was pointing with my finger right toward a carved hand, which had one of its fingers pointing up.

We'd all seen that tombstone before, and we'd all read what was on it, but it was something brand-new on it that had made me gasp. That carved hand with one of its fingers pointing up had never been there before!

We stared at it, and this is what we saw:

SARAH, BELOVED WIFE
OF
SENETH PADDLER

And right above the name was the carved hand, pointing straight toward the top of the tombstone and toward the sky. And at the end of the pointing finger, about an inch above it, was a ribbon-shaped piece of marble with these words carved on it—with brand-new carving, as if it had been done only yesterday:

THERE IS REST IN HEAVEN

All of us felt very sad for a while because we all knew who Seneth Paddler was, and we knew his wife had been dead for a long time, but none of us had ever thought much about his wife. But that new carving meant that the old man still remembered her and was maybe very lonesome for her and wanted to meet her again sometime in heaven.

None of us said anything for a minute, each one of us maybe thinking about what a kind man Old Man Paddler was—that grand old long-whiskered man who liked us so well and whose life we'd once saved. We'd captured the robber that had him all tied and gagged in his cabin up in the hills above the swamp and the old sycamore tree.

Poetry was the first one of us to say anything. I was watching Little Jim's face to see what maybe he was thinking about, and he had a very innocent look, as he nearly always did have. He looked away quick when he saw me looking at him and took a swipe at a goldenrod plume with his stick, just as Poetry spoke up and said, "She was only *thirty-seven* years old." He was especially good in arithmetic.

And Dragonfly said in a voice that sounded like a scared boy's voice coming through a hollow log, "M-my m-mother is just thirty-seven years old."

That started us all talking in kind of low voices about what happened to people when they died and their bodies were buried somewhere.

"They go straight to heaven if they're saved," Little Jim said, and of course he was right. He even quoted a Bible verse to prove it. He knew as many Bible verses as Poetry knew poems. That was the reason he was always piping up and saying things like that. Little Jim was the best Christian in the whole gang.

But when you're in a graveyard, and you know there isn't any such thing as a ghost, and when you all of a sudden get to talking about things like that, you feel kind of spooky anyway.

Maybe it was what Dragonfly said just then that made *me* feel spooky. I don't know, but right after that he said, "My mother saw an actual honest-to-goodness ghost one time, walking right across our front yard at night. It had a crazy voice that sounded like a baby crying and—"

"I don't believe it!" Poetry squawked, interrupting him.

We all agreed with Poetry—all except Dragonfly, of course.

"It could have been one of your dad's white horses," I said, and Circus said with a grin on his monkeylike face, "or one of your lambs or sheep."

Well, we told a few ghost stories to each other until Dragonfly began to look scared. Then we talked about school and our new teacher, Miss Lilly, who was very nice and even pretty for a schoolteacher, and she was so kind. Every single one of us boys liked her.

Pretty soon we were tired of telling ghost stories and also tired of trying to convince Dragonfly that his mom had seen only a white horse or a lamb or a sheep. The word *lamb* reminded Poetry of a poem, which he started to quote in a half-man and half-boy voice, and this is the way the poem went. You know it.

"Mary had a little lamb,
   Its fleece was white as snow,
And everywhere that Mary went,
   The lamb was sure to go.

It followed her to school one day,
   Which was against the rule;
It made the children laugh and play
   To see a lamb at school."

There were several other verses, but the idea was like striking a match to a pile of kerosene-soaked kindling wood. It flared up in our minds, and we decided that, if Poetry wanted to, he could let his pet lamb follow him to school the very next Monday morning.

He would let it follow him to school early, before the teacher came, and he would tie it in the woodshed. Then, maybe along about ten o'clock, he would ask to be excused and would go outdoors and untie the lamb and let it see where he went. We all knew, of course, that it would follow him right into the schoolhouse.

Little Jim didn't exactly like the idea, although there was a mischievous grin on his small face and a twinkle in his sparkling very blue eyes. His eyes were as blue, I thought as I lay there beside him in the tall grass beside Sarah Paddler's tombstone, as blue as the blue sky up there in the direction toward which the finger was pointing.

Well, we brought it to a vote, and the score was seven to none in favor of Poetry's taking his lamb to school Monday morning—none of us knowing that it was going to be a rainy morning and that there would be a mud puddle for the lamb to fall in just a few feet from the schoolhouse door, just before Poetry let it follow him inside.

3

After church the next day and after dinner, which we always have at noon at our house, Poetry and I went riding on our bicycles and learned something else that was important and had to do with the mystery in the cemetery.

Just for fun, we turned into the lane that leads to the cemetery, getting off and walking and pushing our bikes along with us.

After a while we were tired, especially because we were sleepy from having had too much dinner. We leaned our bikes against the rail fence and lay down to rest.

We talked about different things, especially about our Chicago trip by airplane and the terrible electric storm that had been below us when we were high up in the sky, and what that storm had done to things around Sugar Creek while we were gone. We also talked about Dragonfly's experience in the plane when he lost his breakfast because he got dizzy.

"He's always a little dizzy," Poetry squawked.

And just that minute Dragonfly himself came tearing along that abandoned old lane, looking scared—I thought—and running and panting as if a ghost was after him.

"Quick!" he yelled, his voice trembling. "I s-saw it! It's an honest-to-goodness—"

Well, we knew that we were not far from the cemetery, and I guessed that Dragonfly had been up there and had thought he had seen a ghost in the daytime even.

We rolled over in the grass into his way. He stumbled over us, and we had a scramble for a while. It turned out that Dragonfly wasn't scared at all. He was only excited and very happy.

"It's a cave!" he half screamed. "I s-saw it myself with my own eyes!" which, of course, I thought, didn't make it so.

He unscrambled himself from us, jumped to his feet, and started to run, yelling back at us, "Hurry up! Follow me, and I'll show you."

That little spindle-legged guy was so excited that we came to life quick, left our bikes where they were leaning up against the fence, and streaked down the lane after him.

Lickety-sizzle, leap, dodge, whoopee, zip-zip-zip, swish—we followed Dragonfly's flying feet, past the tumbledown old cemetery and over another rail fence. We went sailing down Bumblebee Hill and on toward the spring and to the sycamore tree, which grew on the side of the hill right above Sugar Creek itself.

There Dragonfly stopped and yelled, "Look! See it?"

We looked and panted and couldn't believe what we saw. And yet we had to, because right there it was, a big hole in the side of the hill at the base of the sycamore tree. That old sycamore had been struck by lightning, and there was a great, long, fierce-looking gash running right down the trunk into the ground.

And right there before our eyes we saw that the lightning had opened up an honest-to-goodness cave. As far back inside as we could see, it was still cave and very dark and black, although the entrance was small, just about the size of a boy like Poetry, who, of course, wasn't *small*.

Just that minute I saw somebody's red head push its way out of the cave, and it was Little Tom Till. Then out came Circus's curly brown head and his monkey face; then Big Jim's brown hair and square jaw, followed by Little Jim's blue eyes and mouselike face and mischievous grin—and we were all there.

We found out afterward that Dragonfly had found the cave himself, when he and the rest of the gang had been walking around that afternoon, and they had sent him to hunt up Poetry and me.

Of course Poetry and I wanted to go inside, which we did, and pretty soon all of us were in.

It really wasn't much of a cave, only about ten feet across each way and about seven feet high. But it had a rock wall all around and a rock roof, so we knew it would be a safe place for us to play and wouldn't cave in on us, as a dirt roof might. Our parents wouldn't need to worry about us when we played there.

We all knew it wasn't safe to play in a cave with a dirt or a sand roof, because sometimes they caved in and buried boys alive, smothering them to death.

Big Jim had already been home for some candles. He'd set one on each side up on a little ledge of rock and lit them. We looked funny to each other, sitting there in a sort of half circle with the candles flickering and our faces covered with moving shadows.

We were sitting around telling stories and imagining we were pirates when all of a sudden ,Poetry squawked, "Listen! I hear something!"

We all stopped chattering and listened, and we *did* hear something, I thought. And then I *didn't* think it, because everything was quiet again.

Then Big Jim whispered in a spooky voice and with a hideous grin on his face, "It might be a *ghost!*" His voice was half whisper and half growl.

Dragonfly, who was sitting with his back propped against my shoulder, jumped as though he had heard a shot. You know he was the only one of us who believed in ghosts.

Well, it was too nice an afternoon to stay in a dark cave. We had decided to go outside a while and do something else, when Poetry caught my shirt and whispered, "Wait a minute!"

I waited a minute, and he pulled me back inside a little farther, saying, "Ssh! Listen right here against this side of the cave!"

I laid my head against the rock wall, and what I heard was as plain as day. It sounded kind of spooky at first, and—of course, there just wasn't any sense to it—it sounded like somebody pounding with something very far away.

We looked at each other's face in the candlelight—his big round face and my freckled one—and we knew we had discovered something. The noise was like somebody pounding and not with a hammer, either. It was like somebody with a pickax trying to dig his way out of somewhere.

As you maybe know, Poetry was always imagining himself to be a detective, so he whispered to me, "This is a secret, Bill Collins. Promise me you won't tell a soul."

We shook hands in what we called a solemn pledge not to tell anybody what we'd heard.

Then I moved my freckled face over to one of the candles, and Poetry moved his round face toward the other one, and *puff*, out went the two candles in two breaths. In another minute we were outside in the bright sunlight, which was playing and dancing everywhere and making the little wavelets on Sugar Creek sparkle as if they were happy, which maybe they were.

I hadn't been out of the cave more than a moment when I saw Little Jim standing up by the sycamore tree with his ash stick, striking away at some of the loose bark and knocking it off just for fun. I looked at Poetry, and he looked at me, and we sighed at each other.

"You and your great detective ideas!" I said.

"*My* ideas!" he said disgustedly. "Who said it was my idea?"

With that, Poetry grinned at me as if he had known all the time that the pounding was Little Jim with his stick and had been fooling me. Just the same, he put his forefinger up to his pursed lips and quoted from one of his 101 poems:

"Two ears and only one mouth have you,
  The reason I think is clear:
 It teaches, my child, that it will not do
  To talk about all you hear."

We had fun until it got to be late in the afternoon. When Poetry and I and the rest of the gang couldn't think of anything else we wanted to do together, we had a meeting by the sycamore tree. We agreed to meet at the cave next time. We would each bring a blanket or sleeping bag from home and all sleep there overnight —maybe the very next Friday night—if our parents would let us. Then we adjourned, and each one went whichever way he wanted to with whomever he wanted to our different homes.

Poetry and I went together because our bikes were up there beyond Bumblebee Hill waiting for us. Neither one of us knew we were going to run right smack into another interesting experience before we got home.

4

We rambled back toward Bumblebee Hill, puffed our way up to the top, climbed over the old vine-covered rail fence, pushed our way through the chokecherry shrubs, picking and eating some of the dark-purple, winy-flavored, shiny-skinned cherries and getting our lips stained at the same time.

We'd just come to Sarah Paddler's grave, when all of a sudden Poetry gasped and said, "Come here a minute, will you?"

I poked along over to where he was standing and reading something on a very old tombstone. And would you believe it? It said on that stone, which was tall and flat and had a carved picture of the Good Shepherd at the top, leaning out over the edge of a mountain to save a little lonely lamb from falling:

DANIEL, JOHN, AND WILLIAM
Three sons of
Seneth and Sarah Paddler

There had been more on the stone, which the weather had rubbed out, but I remembered Dad had once told me that Old Man Paddler had had three sons a very long time ago, and that they had all died. That was the reason he liked boys so well and maybe was why he was extra kind to the Sugar Creek Gang.

We were standing there looking at the names and feeling and thinking different things, when Poetry said, "I wonder what they died of?"

"I don't know," I said. "Smallpox, maybe," which is a very dangerous contagious disease against which every boy and every girl ought to be vaccinated so they won't get it. Doctors will even do it free for poor people.

I was looking at the name "William" and wondering how old he had been. You know *my* first name is "William."

Just that minute, we heard somebody coming, so we ran down along the fence, climbed over, and flopped down in the grass of the abandoned lane, not far from our bicycles, and watched.

In a minute, we saw a man hobbling along —an old man with long white whiskers and white hair. He was carrying a yardstick in one hand and a sickle and a potted plant of some kind in the other.

"Ssh!" Poetry shushed me when I started to whisper something.

So I shushed, and we both watched.

We knew right away it was Old Man Paddler himself, who had paid for our airplane trip to Chicago, which we'd had week before last, and who had also paid for our camping trip up north, which you already know about.

I was looking through the bottom rails of the fence and through the flannel-like leaves of a big mullein stalk, of which there were maybe a dozen all around us. In fact, I had a mullein leaf in my hand right that minute, and I thought how nice and soft it was and how white the soft hairs on its very green leaves were. And of course I was wondering what Old Man Paddler was doing there.

But he knew what he was doing. He carefully cut the grass and weeds away from the base of the tombstones—from his wife's and from the one that had his boys' names on it—and then he set the potted plant down on his wife's grave. The next thing we knew he was standing there with his black hat hanging on a bush, looking toward the sky, which had clouds in it as white as his hair, and he began to talk out loud to Someone in a trembling old voice.

This is a part of what he said: "Dear Father in heaven . . . in my heart I'm getting lonesome for my boys and my Sarah, and I'm getting very old . . ."

Just then a little whirlwind, which had been coming across the graveyard, rattled and twisted the bushes and blew the old man's hair across his forehead. It also blew away the sound of his words. He was through praying anyway, I guess, for he put his hat back on his head and started doing the strangest thing.

Poetry reached out and touched my hand to be sure I was watching, and I was.

The old man stood his yardstick up against Sarah Paddler's tombstone and began to measure how tall it was. He did the same to the width at the bottom and at the top and in the middle. And he wrote down something in a little notebook like the one I used at school.

Then he looked around in different directions, took his yardstick and sickle, and moved away, winding around among the weeds and through the vervain, some of which still had little blue flower rings around them, through the chokecherries to the fence, and climbed through —almost.

He got his white shirt caught on a barbed wire, and there he was, stuck. He couldn't go backward or forward or sideways, unless he wanted to tear his shirt.

Well, my parents had taught me to be especially kind to all old people, never to make fun of them, and to be very courteous and helpful. So before I thought, I'd called, "Wait a minute, Mr. Paddler. I'll help you!"

The next thing I knew, I was on my bare feet, running toward him. Poetry got there as quick as I did. In a flash we had his shirt loose, and the old man crawled through.

He certainly was grateful. After he had thanked us, he started to go on toward his home, which I knew was up in the hills. It was an old cabin that looked like the one Abraham Lincoln was born in. It had a clapboard roof and different things that made it look what my mom called "romantic."

I noticed just that minute that he had torn a jagged hole about three inches in different directions in his shirt. I also noticed that his old hands were kind of gnarled, like the twisted grain in a block of wood, and I knew it would be hard for him to handle a small needle. So I said, "Mr. Paddler, if you'll come over to our house tomorrow, my mom will be glad to sew up that rip in your shirt."

He tried to stretch his neck around far enough to see his back and couldn't, but he smiled. I couldn't see the smile because of his long beard, but I saw the twinkles in his kind old eyes, and I knew that a man couldn't have twinkles like that in his eyes and keep a straight face.

"Thank you, Bill," he said. Then all of a sudden he frowned, and all the twinkles left his eyes as he said in his trembling voice, "I used to have a boy of my own named Bill. He was just about your age." His voice stopped, and he swallowed something in his throat, then he turned and shuffled away.

We went on toward home ourselves, getting our bikes on the way. Tomorrow, we told each other, we would be having a lot of fun. Tomorrow, Poetry's innocent lamb, whose fleece was white as snow, would follow him to our red schoolhouse, and all the children would laugh and play to see a lamb at school—because it was, of course, against the rule.

"So long," Poetry puffed at my gate when I turned in.

I rode into the barnyard where Dad was just going out to the barn with two big milk pails. Our black-and-white Mixy was following along behind him and mewing like everything, already hungry for her supper.

"Hurry up, Bill!" Dad called cheerfully.

My wristwatch told me I was later than I should have been. We always had to do our chores early on Sundays because we went to church every Sunday night. Nearly all the Sugar Creek Gang's parents did except Dragonfly's. That is why that little balloon-eyed member of our gang didn't know much about the Bible— only what he got from us, and especially from Little Jim.

Just that second I heard somebody whistle up the road. I looked, and it was Poetry, waving a final good-bye, meaning, "Don't forget tomorrow!"

Which I never did—and never will as long as I live.

5

In the middle of the night, I woke up. Lightning was playing around in the sky, and thunder growled in the distance, and that's how there happened to be mud puddles in the lane the next day when I stopped at Poetry's house to get him on my way to school.

Generally I didn't stop for him because I had to go early to get there before the teacher, and open the windows, and maybe do a little dusting. Every evening after school, it was my job to sweep the schoolhouse floor and lock up after the teacher had gone, unless for some reason she stayed longer than I did.

Well, when I got to Poetry's house, there he came, carrying his red lunch box. And right behind him, crowding close and following all around him, was his innocent lamb, with a rope around its neck so it wouldn't get away from him after he'd fed it, which it sometimes would if he didn't watch out.

As you know, our plan was to tie the lamb in the woodshed and lock the door. It happened there was only one key to that door, and we kept it in a special place, which nobody knew about except the teacher and me and—well, I thought I had to tell Poetry so that later on, after school should have started, and he went outdoors, he could get the key, unlock the door, and the lamb would do the rest.

I had on my boots, because mud and water were everywhere, and so did Poetry, but the lamb's mother hadn't taught him anything like that, and by the time we got to school, the lamb was plenty muddy around the feet and legs.

When I saw the great big brown mud puddle not far from our schoolhouse door, which the township trustee, who was Little Jim's dad, would have to have filled with gravel soon, I said to Poetry, "See to it that he doesn't get all splashed up in the puddle, or you'll have to mop the floor."

Poetry grinned and said, standing beside the little soft-eyed woolly lamb and with his own eyes looking just as innocent, "Lambs don't walk in puddles if they can help it. That's why their mothers never make them wear boots."

"Just the same," I said, "I think we ought to make him wipe his feet on the mat here."

I opened the door and picked up the nice brown mat and set it just outside for the lamb to wipe its feet on.

That lamb acted as though it'd been just waiting to jump up on that step, for the second Poetry stepped up, the lamb was right at his heels, walking around in every direction all over the little six-by-eight porch and getting lamb tracks on it.

"Hey!" I yelled to Poetry. "Get him out of there!" which Poetry did, getting *himself* out of there first. As it was, I would have to get the mop and wipe all the mud off.

Well, we got the key, went to the woodshed, and locked the lamb inside. I decided to keep the key in my pocket, so that in case some of the other members of the gang came early to school, they wouldn't accidentally find the key and go in and look at the lamb and maybe let it out.

As soon as the battered old woodshed door was locked, Poetry and I walked back toward the schoolhouse, stopping on the way at the tall, long-handled iron pump to get a drink out of the drinking cups we had in our lunch boxes.

Poetry and I took off our boots and went inside the schoolhouse. I opened the windows to let fresh air go through, and Poetry went to the blackboard and started working on an arithmetic problem that he had been having trouble with the week before.

Pretty soon, after I had dusted the teacher's desk and the globe of the world and was getting ready to sweep up some dust over in a corner I'd missed the last time I'd swept the floor, there was a shadow in the open doorway. I looked up quick, and there was pop-eyed Dragonfly walking in.

"Hey!" I yelled indignantly at him, with my eyebrows down the way my dad's are when he is angry at something or somebody or me.

Dragonfly stood stock-still. "'S'matter?" he called. "Where's the lamb?"

"Listen, you!" I exclaimed, waving my broom

at him and starting toward him on the half run. "You get yourself out of here and wipe your feet on the mat—or out on the grass *first* and then the mat—and keep *still* about the lamb!"

Dragonfly obeyed as meekly as an innocent lamb is supposed to. Then he came back in and walked between the rows of seats and around the big Poetry-shaped iron stove in the middle of the room.

Finally he stopped in front of our seven-inch-thick dictionary, which always lies open or shut on a low shelf on the south wall near a window. He started looking up different words, while Poetry kept working away with noisy chalk on the blackboard and I kept on sweeping a little, dusting, and acting important, and feeling the same way.

All of a sudden, Dragonfly said, "My mom saw another ghost last night!"

I stopped sweeping and said saucily, "Stop saying stuff like that! You know there isn't any such thing as a ghost."

And Dragonfly replied equally as saucily as I had, "You know it, and I know it, but my *mother* doesn't know it. Say, come here, will you?" he raised his voice excitedly.

In a jiffy Poetry and I were beside him, Poetry dropping an eraser and a piece of chalk on the way, and I stopping to pick up the broom I'd just dropped.

"See here!" Dragonfly said. "Here's what it says a ghost is!"

I looked at the place where his crooked fingernail was pointing, and it said: "Ghost, *noun*, 1. A disembodied spirit."

"What's *disembodied* mean?" Dragonfly wanted to know, and for a second I knew he was believing the same thing his mother believed.

I sighed and looked at Poetry, who, as he had done yesterday, put his forefinger up to his lips and said, "'Two ears and only one mouth have you.'"

Poetry interrupted himself then and said, "Here, let's look up the word *disembodied,*" which he did, and pretty soon my blue-gray eyes and Poetry's sky-blue ones and Dragonfly's brown balloon-shaped ones were all looking at the definition of the word *disembody,* and Poetry's squawky voice was reading.

"*Verb, transitive,* to free from the body."

And that meant a ghost was a spirit free from its body.

"See there!" Dragonfly said triumphantly. "It doesn't say there *isn't* any such thing!"

No, it didn't, and I was remembering the pounding noise I'd heard in the cave yesterday, which might have been Little Jim's stick against the old sycamore tree and probably was.

Well, pretty soon Miss Lilly would be there and, a little later, the rest of the seventeen pupils who came to our little red brick schoolhouse.

Even though it had rained hard during the night, the sun was out now. It was going to be a very cheerful day—and hard for us to keep the grins off when we thought of the lamb that was locked up out in the woodshed and would stay there until Poetry went to let it out.

And then we heard a car. It was Miss Lilly herself in her green coupe, stopping right under the big sugar tree not far from the tall, long-handled pump.

She sort of *looked* like a lily that morning, I thought, as she stepped out onto the grass-covered ground. Her pretty, long brown hair was very carefully combed the way Little Jim's mom combed hers. She was wearing a brown-and-white dress, the white being kind of lily designs. She had several books and a lunch basket, which, as quick as we could get to her car, Poetry and Dragonfly and I offered to carry into the schoolhouse.

"Good morning, boys!" her musical voice said to us very cheerfully, and she smiled at us in a way that made me desire to study hard all day—that is, as soon as I could after the lamb had come in.

At that minute I heard a sound coming from the woodshed as though something was trying to get out the door. I also heard a lamb bleating.

I could feel my hair acting funny under my cap, and I could see Poetry's face turn red and Dragonfly's eyes get bigger.

Miss Lilly looked around quickly and exclaimed, "What was *that?*"

And Poetry squawked indifferently, looking at me before I could look away. "That—that was probably a—maybe some new kind of bird singing. There's always some new bird around."

Miss Lilly laughed and said, "You always have an answer, don't you, Poetry? It is a nice day, isn't it?" Then she started toward the door of the school, with us carrying the different things for her.

Whew! I thought. *That was a close shave!* She had actually heard the lamb, and she could have also seen the little cloven-foot tracks there in the mud too, if she had looked, but she hadn't.

Well, right after that, children started to come from different directions, some across the fields, some down the lane, and others on the road. Pretty soon our gang was all there, which was all the boys there were in our school. The rest of the children were just girls, some big and some little and most of them with different-colored and different-sized hair ribbons in their different-colored hair, and all of them carrying lunch boxes and some of them books.

They all came through the little wooden gate not far from the tall, long-handled iron pump, playing and saying different things to each other, most of them being noisy, except for a few very bashful girls who were coming to school for the very first time that year.

Big Jim was standing right beside me when Sylvia's little sister came walking through the gate. Sylvia, you know, is our minister's oldest daughter. She had been in the eighth grade the year before and was going to town to high school this year. Big Jim had had to stay out of school one whole year before he moved into Sugar Creek territory a few years ago, because he had had an operation. So he was still in eighth grade, for which we were very glad.

All of a sudden, Sylvia's little sister, Jeanelle, came sidling up to Big Jim with her pigtails flopping down on her neck and handed him something that I guessed was a note. Big Jim shoved it into his pocket quick and started whistling and walking off across the schoolyard by himself, yawning and acting indifferent and stretching his arms lazily.

Soon the last bell rang, and all of us who were outside went storming in—that is, we went like lions up to as far as the door, then we went inside like a lot of lambs. Just as we got to the door, I slipped the woodshed key to Poetry, who shoved it into one of his pockets and went innocently to his seat across the room from me. The smallest kids sat in the front seats near the teacher's desk. In a few moments everybody was quiet.

First thing on the program was "opening exercises," which lasted for ten minutes and was the reading of an interesting Bible story out of a children's Bible storybook and then a short prayer by Miss Lilly herself, with all of us bowing our heads reverently. Then we started off the day's work, studying and reciting and keeping quiet, which is harder even than hard work unless you are *interested* in your work.

The first grade did some slow, monotonous reading, which made it hard for me to study. In a one-room schoolhouse you have to study most of the time while somebody else is talking.

That was especially hard for me, for just that minute I was looking at an arithmetic problem that said, "Mr. Brown had 37 sheep whose wool averaged 7 pounds each. He sold the wool at $1.00 per pound and deposited one-half of the money in the State Bank, one-third of it in the Security Bank, and paid his lumber bill with the remaining sum. How much was his lumber bill?"

I looked out of the corner of my eye at Poetry, who was looking at me out of the corner of *his* eye, and he snickered because he was trying to work the same arithmetic problem I was.

· But when Miss Lilly turned around from the blackboard, our faces were as blank as the sheet of paper I was supposed to be working problems on, as also was Poetry's.

Well, we suffered along for ten or fifteen minutes, each one of the Sugar Creek Gang, even Little Jim, acting very busy. Then all of a sudden Poetry raised one of his big hands and asked to be excused.

Miss Lilly looked at him in the blank way teachers do when they are thinking about something else and nodded her brown head absentmindedly.

Poetry turned sideways, set his feet in the aisle, stood up, and started walking heavily, because his feet are big and he is very heavy himself, toward the only door the schoolhouse had. He pushed open the screen and went out.

I kept my face straight and my eyes on my arithmetic, trying to figure out how much Mr. Brown owed the lumberyard and how many pounds of wool his thirty-seven sheep had. I frowned and scowled at that problem and at the thousand or more snickers that were trying to burst out of my mouth.

Some of the windows were still open. I heard Poetry walking toward the woodshed, then I heard the rattle of a steel lock, and I even thought I heard the sound of the key turning in the lock. Then I heard the door swing open, *squeak-squeak-squeak.*

Why on earth, I thought, *didn't we think to oil that woodshed door?*

And then, a little later, I heard a lot of steps coming toward the schoolhouse on the gravel just outside the door.

I was close to the window, so I took a quick sideways glance and saw that Poetry looked worried. I supposed he had lost his nerve and was trying to get the lamb to change its mind about following him inside. The lamb was all around him and in front of him and behind him and then—

Well, I heard water splashing, and I knew what *that* meant—with a mud puddle not far from the schoolhouse door. Right away I heard steps on the porch, the door opening, and a scuffling noise. And the next thing I knew, there was Poetry coming in and trying to keep the lamb out—or pretending to. I couldn't tell which.

And then the lamb was inside. Inside! A lamb in our schoolhouse! A *muddy* lamb with very muddy feet!

6

Mary had a little lamb,
  Its fleece was white as snow,
And everywhere that Mary went,
  The lamb was sure to go.

It followed her to school one day—
  Which was against the rule;
It made the children laugh and play
  To see a lamb at school.

And so the teacher put him out . . .

That's the way the poem goes, and it certainly sounds like an innocent little jingle, but
when you try to act it out in real life as we did—
well, it certainly wasn't.

Somebody ought to rewrite that poem and
make it say something like this:

Poetry had a little lamb,
  Its fleece a dirty black;
The only place its wool was white
  Was high upon its back.

It followed him to school one day,
  It made the teacher sick,

I couldn't study geography,
　　Nor get my 'rithmetic.

The children didn't laugh or play,
　　It made them stare and blush,
And over all that one-room school
　　There came an awful hush.

And Big Jim, Little Jim, and Tom,
　　And Circus too, and me
And Dragonfly—the six of us—
　　Were scared as Poetry.

Something like that would make a good start for a poem that would be more true to life than the one about Mary's innocent lamb.

There wasn't anything innocent about *our* lamb that day. The very minute it and Poetry got inside, it began to act wild. It started running around in different directions, scared and bleating, making muddy tracks everywhere and making the little girls cry. It upset a mop bucket that was by the door under the long shelf where the lunch boxes sat all in a row. That bucket went banging and rolling and emptying its soapy water in different directions all over the floor.

And that's how I happened to have to stay in at recess to clean up the whole mess. In fact, we had recess right away, a nice long one for everybody except some of us.

Quick as a flash, when that pail of soapy water was turned over, different ones of us raised our feet fast as the water came toward us, like a farmer getting his chickens and hogs out of the way when Sugar Creek goes on a rampage.

Miss Lilly called us to order, saying, "All right, everybody! Quiet, please!"

She stood there behind her desk like a queen, her face saying there was going to be some kind of trouble but not saying what.

As soon as we all quieted down, the lamb did the same thing. And Miss Lilly said to Poetry very sternly, "Leslie, will you please open the door and lead the animal out!"

Leslie "Poetry" Thompson was as meek as a lamb was supposed to be. He stood to his big feet and said politely, "Yes, ma'am!" He walked heavily to the door and opened it.

The lamb all of a sudden saw him and got there almost as quick as he did—and got out even quicker, making a noise as it scampered across the porch and out onto the gravel walk.

Glancing around quick, I saw it stop and lift its head and look back up to the door at Poetry.

After that, Miss Lilly said to all the rest of us, "There will be a short recess for everyone except the boys. Go quietly, please. Turn."

The girls turned, setting their feet out in the aisles, each one trying to miss the soapy water.

Then Miss Lilly said, "Stand," and they stood and waited for her to say, "Pass," which she did, and they went out very quietly, walking as if they were walking on eggs that might break any minute.

The second the last girl was out, Miss Lilly went to the door and shut it and walked back to the front of the room. She stood beside her desk with one hand resting on the top of the globe. Her face was sober, and it looked as if the whole world was going to be against us. We didn't know what to expect, and my heart was pounding.

Little Jim, who was sitting across the aisle from me, was even white, he was so tense inside. Poetry for once in his life didn't look mischievous. And Circus didn't have any tree he could climb to let off some of the extra steam that was almost all the time inside him trying to get out.

Dragonfly looked as if he was seeing one of his mother's ghosts. Little Tom Till's freckled face and red hair looked the way they always did—his face a little dirty, his hair a little mussed up in different places, especially at the top of the back where he had a cowlick, which means a place where the hair starts growing in different directions. It actually does look like a place on a calf's back that our old brindle cow has just licked with her rough tongue.

Big Jim looked very calm, though. He had one hand in his pocket, where probably the note was that Sylvia's little sister had given him, I thought.

Miss Lilly stood for a long time with her hand on the world. I could tell she was thinking what to do with us and couldn't decide. There was a very pretty sparkling ring on her hand, which looked like a diamond, and I noticed that Big Jim was looking at it and admiring it and maybe wasn't thinking about any muddy lamb.

Then Miss Lilly cleared her throat, which didn't need clearing, and said to Poetry, "Leslie, will you step outside, please, and bring your lamb in again?"

He stared at her until she said firmly, *"Now,* please!"

Poetry walked to the door, looked out, and called the lamb by name, which was "Jerry," and the lamb, seeing him, was on the steps right away. Then Poetry and the lamb were inside again.

And that lamb, even though it was still dirty, was as meek as could be. It even let Miss Lilly put her hand on it, stroking it, letting her hand move from its forehead across its poll, which is its head, and down its neck to its withers, which is the part of a lamb where its neck and back meet.

Of course, Poetry had to stand beside her and the lamb to make it stay there, but it acted as if it liked to have her stroke it—just as a kitten purrs to show you it *really* does.

Well, I knew by the expression that came into Miss Lilly's soft blue eyes that she wasn't going to scold us.

Instead, her voice got a faraway expression in it, just as her eyes had, and she said, "Boys, members of the Sugar Creek Gang, I wonder if you remember the story of a man named John who lived a long time ago in a beautiful little country right in the very center of the world, known now as Palestine. He was speaking one day to a large crowd of people who had come out along a river to listen to him. This John was a prophet of the God who made the whole world. He had just finished preaching a sermon, when all of a sudden, Someone came walking along the river, a strong young Man whose life was clean and pure and who had never done a wrong thing in His life.

"That young Man, strong and pure in mind and body, walked toward John before all the people. Seeing Him, John raised his great voice and cried out to the people, 'Behold, the Lamb of God who takes away the sin of the world!'"

And then Miss Lilly lowered her voice, but her face still had that very quiet, faraway look on it as she said, stroking the little lamb's head and neck, "That young Man was the only Man in all the history of the world who could have taken away . . . taken away . . ."

Then Miss Lilly's faraway voice stopped speaking. She looked at each one of us as though she wasn't seeing us, and she very gently stroked the head and forehead of the lamb with one hand, looking at it quietly. Then she turned her pretty face and looked across to the globe of the world, where her other hand was resting, and there were tears in her eyes when she decided to go on.

"That young Man's name was the Lord Jesus Christ. He is the One of whom John the

Baptist said, 'Behold, the Lamb of God who takes away the sin of the world.'"

I looked across to Little Jim, sitting with his little hands in front of him on the top of his desk. His eyes were glued to Miss Lilly, and his fists were doubled up. I thought I saw him swallow something in his throat.

Circus was sitting with his hands on his knees under the desk. Tom Till had his feet out in the aisle but was leaning forward sideways with his chin resting on the back of his hands and his elbows on the desk. Poetry was moving one of his hands around in his desk, feeling for something, which he soon found, and it was his New Testament. He started to open it right away and look up the story Miss Lilly had just told us.

Big Jim and I weren't doing anything except listening, but something very strange was going on in my mind. All the time she was talking so kindly, I kept thinking of the One she was talking about, and I kept looking at the big round world, which had millions of people on it who didn't even know yet that Somebody had died for their sins. And I wished everybody who knew about it would hurry up and tell everybody else. I even wished I could tell a lot of people myself. I forgot all about the mischievous prank the Sugar Creek Gang had just played.

Right that minute, while those different thoughts were splashing around in my mind, Miss Lilly said, raising her voice, "And now, Leslie, if you will put your lamb out to pasture, and if you, Bill, will get busy with the mop and pail, we'll have the schoolhouse ready for business in a few minutes."

No punishment? I thought. *No scolding?*

But there wasn't. Not even a frown. And do you know what? Just that quick, I decided I liked our new teacher very much, and someday when I got big enough, I was going to be a very special friend of somebody just like her and protect her from all kinds of danger, such as wolves howling at night, or some gangster, or save her from drowning or something. And if she was afraid of a spider or a mouse, as most girls and even women are, I'd kill one of them for her too.

Well, all the Sugar Creek Gang went to work on that schoolhouse floor, and in almost less than no time it was ready for occupation. The bell rang, and the girls came back in, all of them looking at us.

School started again and went on as usual, with nothing important happening until noon that day.

The gang was lying out in the shade of a big ash tree at the west end of our schoolyard, and Big Jim pulled a folded piece of paper out of his pocket and read it to us. It was the note Sylvia's little sister had given him in the morning. And what that note said was plenty!

Plenty!

7

We were all lying under the ash tree, with our heads together and our bodies resting in seven different directions like a human wheel with seven spokes. The lower end of each spoke divided like the fork of a boy's slingshot, and there wasn't any rim on the wheel, and some of the spokes were shorter than some of the others.

Big Jim opened the note and asked us to get ready to listen to something important. And it wasn't from Sylvia at all but was printed in somebody's awkward style, maybe a boy's, and whoever had done it had used a purple indelible pencil, probably wetting the pencil with a sponge or something. Or if he didn't know better, he might have done it with his tongue. Indelible pencil is poison, you know, if you wet it that way.

Well, I was watching the almost imaginary fuzz on Big Jim's upper lip while he was talking and getting ready to read.

This is what the note said:

Just to warn you that the cave at the base of the old sycamore tree is haunted. So please STAY AWAY!

I don't know what made me do it, but all of a sudden I lifted my eyes and looked at Dragonfly. He was acting a little funny, I thought. His eyes were big, the way they always are, and he looked very innocent. But just that second, I looked under his crooked nose, which turns south at the end, and I saw with my own eyes a little bit of purple marking on his teeth, which were too big for his small face and would be until his face grew some more.

I looked from Dragonfly's funny face to Poetry's round one, and Poetry was already looking at my freckled one. He winked at me, and I remembered the pounding noise he and I had heard the day before in the cave. I'd even thought there had been the sound of water running, like from a small underground spring. I also remembered his poem about not talking about all you see and hear.

There was no name signed to the note, I noticed. So did the rest of us, and right that minute our nice wagon wheel with its seven divided spokes got broken up, and all of us sat in an interested huddle around Big Jim.

Such crazy printing I had never seen, and the note was so short that it almost made me feel creepy. *What if the cave* is *haunted?* I thought. What if Dragonfly's mother had been right?

And then I felt Little Jim's hand catch hold of my suspender as though he was glad to have something to hold onto, and I knew that even though he *knew* there wasn't any such thing as a ghost, he still wondered if there might not be maybe just *one!*

Just that minute also, I clapped my hand over my mouth to stop myself from asking Big Jim, "How come Sylvia's little sister, Jeanelle, gave the note to you?" I would ask that later, I thought.

We sat there talking and still talking, saying there wasn't any such thing as a ghost and Dragonfly saying there *might* be.

Every now and then I saw the purple on his two big incisors, which is the name of the two biggest front teeth a boy has. But I decided to keep still for a while and talk it over with Poetry later.

We talked a little about the lamb at school, and we also watched the girls who were walking around on the other side of the schoolyard. Circus did a few acrobatic stunts on a strong limb of the ash tree, which hung down close to the ground. And then Big Jim said, "Let's have a meeting."

We gathered around him in a tangled-up circle, some of us on our elbows, and some of us on our knees and on each other's elbows and knees.

Big Jim said, "Will someone make a motion to the effect that we have a meeting at the cave next Friday night—that is, that we take our sleeping bags and sleep in the cave just to show the ghosts that there aren't any?"

We looked at each other, and then most of us looked at Dragonfly, and I said to that pop-eyed person, nodding my red head to him at the same time, "Go ahead and make the motion."

"I will not," he said, and I saw the purple stains on his teeth again.

"You're a scaredy-cat," Poetry said to him, and Big Jim's voice said gruffly, "Order, please!" and there was.

Just then Circus said, "I move we sleep in the cave next Friday night."

"Second the motion," I said.

"Third it," Poetry squawked.

Big Jim said, "Order," again. Then he said, "It has been moved and seconded that we, all of us including Dragonfly, sleep in the cave next Friday night. Are you ready for the question?"

We were, so he said, "All in favor, please respond by the uplifted hand."

Dragonfly cut in then and said, "You forgot to ask if there were any remarks."

Big Jim frowned and said, "Well, *are* there any? Anybody afraid to sleep in a cave—an innocent cave?"

Nobody was, and the motion carried, which means that most of us voted yes. Sitting and lying and sprawling there on the long grass, each one of us, except Dragonfly, had his hand up, although I couldn't help but notice that Little Jim's hand wasn't very high. His fingers were pressed tight together, and his hand was very close to his face, right beside his right blue eye, which had a hollow look in it. Tom Till waited till the rest of us had voted yes before he did the same thing.

Pretty soon we heard the school bell ring. Then we all, the whole school of seventeen, started running lickety-sizzle toward that one-room schoolhouse's only door, which was painted a kind of blue-gray and had a white knob, which had to be washed often to *keep* it white.

I couldn't help but remember the time I had been up north on our camping trip, fishing for bluegills with a worm and had looked down into the blue-gray water under the boat. *Wow!* The minute the worm went down, down, down, about seventeen different sizes and kinds of fish had darted toward it—the worm *and* the hook—perch, bluegills, rock bass, and others.

Poetry and I stayed behind a little, and on the way I said, "Did you notice Dragonfly's teeth?"

"Sure," he said. "They're big enough to eat up Little Red Riding Hood's grandmother."

"I mean," I explained, "did you notice their color? There were indelible pencil stains on them."

"What!" he said and stood stock-still.

"Actually," I said.

Just that minute, his lamb, which had been lying peacefully under the big maple tree near the long-handled iron pump, raised its innocent head and started toward us at a half run, with its tail flapping along behind it. That reminded Poetry of a poem, which right away he started to quote and which made us both a little late for school. The poem was:

Little Bo-Peep has lost her sheep,
    And can't tell where to find them;
Leave them alone and they'll come home,
    Bringing their tails behind them.

He stood with one of his big hands resting on the lamb's poll, and he looked down at it as if it was his best friend. He said to it, "Little innocent lamb, you'd make a very innocent white ghost next Friday night."

With that, Poetry looked at me, winked, and put a forefinger up to his pursed lips.

Then we both realized that Miss Lilly was standing at the school door, holding it open for us to hurry up and get through before we were too late.

Well, I got busy and found out how much Mr. Brown's lumber bill was so he could pay it. But the afternoon moved along slowly, and I realized that it was going to be a slow week. I wanted next Friday night to come right that very minute so I could take my sleeping bag and sleep in the Sugar Creek cave.

At half past two in the afternoon of that Monday, we had recess, which lasts fifteen short minutes that seem only about five. As soon as I got a chance, I talked to Big Jim alone.

I said to him, "How come Sylvia's little sister gave the note to you? Where'd she get it, and who wrote it?"

Of course, I knew Dragonfly had written it, because he had indelible pencil stain on his teeth, and he was the only one who was afraid of ghosts. Besides, that very morning he had stood in front of our big school dictionary and looked up the word "ghost" for us.

Big Jim looked down at me with an embarrassed expression on his face and said, "Who told you that?"

"I saw her give it to you," I said.

Big Jim looked funny for a minute. Then he said, "If you *have* to know, I gave it to Sylvia last night in church to see what she thought about it, and she sent it back with Jeanelle this morning."

We were standing by ourselves under the big ash tree. The rest of the school, including even the girls, was at the other end of the yard playing prisoner's base and hollering and making a lot of ordinary noise.

"Where'd you get the note in the first place?" I asked.

And he said, "Dragonfly gave it to me."

Just that minute, there was the sound of somebody sneezing behind the tree. I looked, and a part of Poetry was showing on one side of the big tree and the other side of him was showing on the other side, which shows how big the tree actually was.

Big Jim looked around quick, and that's how Poetry happened to get in on our talk. We had to invite him, because he'd heard us.

"And where did *Dragonfly* get the note?" Poetry asked. He winked at me secretly.

Big Jim said, "Little Jim gave it to him."

"Little Jim!" Poetry and I exclaimed in a duet.

"What's so funny about that?" Big Jim asked.

"Nothing," I said, "but where'd *Little Jim* get it?"

"Found it," Big Jim said, and his face was sober. "Found it on their car floor."

"On their car floor!" Poetry and I exclaimed in another duet.

Just then the two-minute bell rang, which meant we'd all better get ready to make a dive for the schoolhouse door as soon as the last bell should ring, as it did almost right away.

As usual, Poetry and I walked and ran together, and just as we went whizzing past the lamb, he said to me, "Dragonfly didn't write that note."

"Why not?" I puffed.

"'Cause Big Bob Till did."

I stopped running and walking, stood still, and said, "Bob Till is still in Chicago!"

I was remembering the excitement we'd had there over Labor Day weekend, which you already know about if you've read my story about the Sugar Creek Gang in Chicago. I also remembered that Tom's brother, Big Bob, who had been arrested in Chicago, had been paroled to Little Jim's dad.

Big Bob Till, as you know, was the leader of a tough gang of town boys whom we'd licked the daylights out of last year in the famous Battle of Bumblebee Hill near the old cemetery.

Bob had stolen some money from our grocer's store, had run away to Chicago, had been arrested, and would have been in jail right that minute, I thought, if Little Jim's dad hadn't been willing to have him paroled to him.

"No," Poetry said just as we zipped up to the school porch, "Big Bob came home Saturday afternoon in Little Jim's dad's car."

8

*S*o! I thought. *Big Bob Till is home again.* The ugly-faced boy whose father was not a Christian. The boy who hadn't been to church in his whole life, and who was always causing trouble for the Sugar Creek Gang, and who was the leader of that tough gang of town boys who called themselves "The Hellfire Gang."

All the rest of the afternoon we kept thinking about him. I say "we" because Poetry sent a note over to me, and he shouldn't have, and the note said:

After school let's go down to the cave and go in and listen again.

I quickly folded the note and shoved it into one of my five pants pockets just before Miss Lilly looked around from the blackboard where she had been working a problem for Dragonfly.

As soon as school was out and all seventeen students had gone except Poetry and me—who stayed to sweep the floor and close the windows and finally lock the door after Miss Lilly left—Poetry and I went down the lane to my house. His pet lamb was following and bringing its tail behind it.

"Home early today?" Mom asked when I

rushed into the kitchen to set my lunch box on a shelf in the corner.

"Yep," I said. "Poetry stayed and helped me so I could help him with something he wanted to do after school. Can I? I mean, can I go over to Poetry's house or somewhere to help him do something?"

Mom, who was sitting in the living room and working on a small dress for Charlotte Ann, looked up and talked with a pin in her mouth. "Why, yes, I guess so. Except that your father is expecting you to take this shirt up to Old Man Paddler's cabin for him. He brought it to me this morning, saying you told him to. I've patched it the best I can."

She got up from her rocker and carefully wrapped the shirt in a piece of paper and gave it to me. Mom had not only sewed up the jagged rip but had washed and ironed the shirt as well, which shows what kind of a mom I've got and also how much she liked Old Man Paddler.

"Here," she said. "Take these to him too." With that, she went to the pantry to our cookie jar and took out two dozen fresh raisin cookies and put them in a brown paper sack just as Poetry —who was out on the back porch—cleared his husky throat.

"Why, hello, Poetry," Mom exclaimed. "Would you like a cookie?"

"Of course—I mean, certainly. Thank you," Poetry said politely, always being especially polite at a time like this.

It didn't take us long to get started through

the woods to Old Man Paddler's house up in the hills. Poetry was carrying the shirt, and I the cookies.

We had to go past the old sycamore tree to get to the path that led to the old man's cottage. When we got there, we stopped at the cave to rest because the weather was still hot.

We laid the cookies and the shirt in the hole in the tree, and both of us crawled slowly in through the cave entrance and sat down inside. The late afternoon sun shone in and made it almost light inside.

Just to give it atmosphere, we lit one of the candles and then sat a while, noticing how nice and dry it was and what a fine place it was going to be for sleeping there next Friday night—if our parents would let us.

We listened as hard as we could, to see if we could hear the strange pounding noise we'd heard the day before. But we didn't—not at first. We did hear running water coming from somewhere, though, but it was faraway sounding, and we decided maybe it was an underground stream somewhere. You know there are millions of little underground streams in the earth, like arteries and veins running through a boy's body.

"Listen!" Poetry exclaimed squawkily into my ear, startling me. "Hear it? There it is again. That pounding noise."

I listened, and, sure enough, there it was, the same pounding we'd heard the day before, like somebody with a pickax digging far back in the earth. I tell you, I felt creepy.

The next thing we knew we were both outside, looking all around to see if we could see anybody or anything, and we couldn't. One thing I did see with my mind's eyes was the purple stains on Dragonfly's front teeth. And in my imagination, I also saw the scribbled note that told us the cave was haunted.

"I don't believe it!" Poetry said. But, for the first time in a long time, he had a worried expression on his face. "There isn't such a thing as a ghost."

We listened outside and didn't hear anything, so we went inside again to blow out the candle.

"Maybe it was our imagination," I said.

Poetry said, "Absolutely not! But I don't believe it anyway."

Just the same, it was spooky in that cave, so we got out, took our cookies and the shirt, and went on. Poetry carried the cookies this time.

Pretty soon, as we climbed the hill, he said, "How many cookies did you say were in this sack?"

"Twenty-four," I answered. I'd seen Mom count them and put them in a long row in the bottom of the sack.

"There's twenty-five," Poetry said, holding open the sack and looking in.

We walked on a while, and then he said, "Did you say there were *supposed* to be only twenty-four?"

"Maybe the ghost put in an extra one while we were in the cave," I said.

Poetry grunted and replied, "Any sensible ghost would have taken one *out,* rather than put one in."

I agreed with him.

Just the same, we had a tingling feeling inside all the way up to Old Man Paddler's cabin, thinking and talking about what made the pounding noise and wondering if it had been our imagination or not.

Just then Poetry stopped again, so suddenly that I bumped *kersquash* into him. "Ssh! Listen!"

I listened, and there it was again, the same pounding sound I'd heard before. This time it was right ahead of us. In fact, it was coming from the direction of Old Man Paddler's cabin.

Poetry and I looked at each other's face. Then we looked at the cabin again.

Out in the yard was the long-whiskered old man himself, chopping kindling on a block of wood, which was on a big slab of rock behind his house.

That settled that, I thought, and so did Poetry. We hadn't heard any ghost because there weren't any in the whole world.

"I'm mad!" Poetry exclaimed.

"Why?" I asked.

"Because," Poetry answered. "I really wanted there to be a ghost—even if there isn't any such thing."

Well, just that minute the old man saw us

coming. He straightened up, stood his ax against the block of wood, and said in his kind old voice, "Good afternoon, Poetry. Good afternoon, Bill."

"We brought your shirt," I said, holding out the package.

Poetry said, "And two dozen cookies from Bill's mom—I mean, Mrs. Collins."

"Well, well," the old man said with sunshine in his voice. "Come on in the house a while, and I'll get you something to take back with you." He carried the shirt in one hand and the sack of cookies in the other.

We followed him inside and sat down on a couple of homemade wooden chairs.

Old Man Paddler walked to the trapdoor in his floor, lifted it up, and went down into his cellar.

The minute his white hair disappeared into that dark hole, I remembered the time he had fallen down that same stairway and had hurt his leg. He would maybe have frozen to death if our gang hadn't come to his cabin that day and saved his life.

I remembered, too, that it wasn't much of a cellar—about ten feet square.

Well, I was sitting there feeling proud of myself and the gang to think that we'd saved his life, when Poetry—who was sitting on half of his chair—jumped, lost his balance, and went *kersquash* on the floor.

"'S'matter?" I asked.

He was almost white. He looked at me,

then picked himself up off the floor and said, "Did you hear *that*?" His voice had a husky whisper in it.

"Hear what?"

"A door slam shut!"

I looked at him and said, "You're getting to be like Dragonfly—scared of ghosts."

"I-I a-am not! But I did hear a door slam somewhere!"

"What of it?" I asked, scolding him. "Can't a door slam without giving you the jitters? That was the wind maybe, blowing the woodshed door shut."

I looked out the window. The woodshed door was wide open and propped open with a stick, and besides that, the wind wasn't blowing.

Just that minute Old Man Paddler's white head and long beard came up the cellar steps. He had in his hand a little box full of reddish-colored pieces of wood that looked like a lot of chips from our woodpile at home.

Sassafras roots, I thought, remembering that Little Jim always liked sassafras tea so well.

Mr. Paddler shut the trapdoor, with both of us helping a little. Then he said, "If you aren't in a hurry, I'll make some tea, and we can have a little party with your cookies."

But we were supposed to be in a hurry, so he didn't urge us to stay. He opened the sack of cookies, though, and put them on a plate. Then he put the sassafras roots in the paper bag for us to take home, half for Poetry's parents and the other half for mine.

I counted the cookies while he was taking them out, and there were exactly twenty-four, just as my mom had said there would be in the first place.

"Your arithmetic is getting worse," I said to Poetry. "There are just twenty-four. You can't count straight."

He grinned and said, "I'm still good at subtraction." Then he grinned again and started whistling to himself. I never did find out what he meant or why he had that mischievous look in his eye.

The minute we got out the door, ready to start down the little hill toward the spring where the old man got his drinking water, Poetry turned around quick and said, "Mr. Paddler, do you believe in ghosts?"

9

We might have known the old man didn't believe in ghosts or disembodied spirits hanging around this world, making pounding noises in caves or slamming doors. He explained why he didn't believe in them, and we started on home.

We followed the winding old wagon trail partway and then cut off and went through the swamp to save time. Just as we started to disappear into the thick woods, we heard a car coming in low gear up the trail. Looking down, we saw a beautiful green coupe, and we knew right away whose it was.

"Miss Lilly!" Poetry and I exclaimed under our breath and ducked down behind some second growth oaks to hide until the car went purring past.

"What's she doing going up to Old Man Paddler's?" Poetry asked me.

"I don't know," I said, but I felt myself liking both of them at the same time, thinking maybe if Miss Lilly had been the old man's daughter, she would have had a very nice father.

Then Poetry and I hurried along, stopping only for a jiffy at the cave and listening but not hearing anything. We went on to Poetry's house, each one of us thinking and talking—feeling fine, because we did not believe there was any such thing as a ghost—and pleased that we were going to sleep in the cave that Friday night, if our parents would let us.

"We must not tell our folks we think we've heard anything," I said to Poetry, "or they'll be afraid to let us sleep there."

"Or else they'll laugh at us for being superstitious," Poetry panted.

We'd been running hard for a minute because we felt so good. We stopped at his gate to catch our breath.

"There just isn't any sense to what we thought we heard," Poetry said, and there wasn't.

Well, it was time for me to go home and help Dad with the chores, so I told Poetry, "So long," which means, "Good-bye for a while," or else, "It will be just so long until we see each other again."

It was while I was up in our haymow throwing down forkfuls of alfalfa hay for our horses and cows that I heard my dad downstairs talking to somebody, so I listened, and it was Old Man Paddler!

How in the world! I thought. *How did he get here so quick?* Why, that old man had to walk with a cane, and he certainly couldn't walk as fast as Poetry and I could—although I suppose I did get home a little later because I had stopped at Poetry's house. *But then, of course, he could have ridden with Miss Lilly in her car,* I thought.

"No," my dad's big half-gruff voice said. "I

don't think there is any use to try. The law is the law, and that settles it. I do hate to see a boy have to go to reform school for his first offense, though."

Then Old Man Paddler's trembling voice came floating up to me, sounding kind of like a screech owl's voice does at night as he said, "I keep thinking, what if it was my William that was in trouble?"

"I know, I know," Dad's big voice answered.

And then my dad said something that made me feel creepy all over and made me wonder what was going to happen. It also made me a little angry.

My dad said, "Well, I'll have a talk with him and see if I can get him to change his ways."

What! I thought. *Are they talking about* me?

"Thank you, Mr. Collins," Old Man Paddler said. "That will help, I am sure. Maybe it's just a whim of an old man, but I believe it's worth trying. Some of the world's greatest men have been made of bad-boy material. If I remember right, you were active yourself when you were only a little red-haired—" His voice was lost as one of our cows let out a very sorrowful bawl.

I stood there in the haymow, feeling hot inside, and worried, and wondering what I'd done wrong. I couldn't think of anything except the lamb at school and my having given the woodshed key to Poetry and helping him to do his mischievous prank.

Both my dad's voice and Old Man Paddler's were getting fainter, so I knew they were walking away. I peeped through a crack between the weatherboarding of the barn and saw them walking toward our house, my dad's bushy reddish-brown hair and the old man's white hair side by side, with the going-down sun shining on them.

They stopped right under the crossbeam that goes over our grape arbor, near our iron pitcher pump, and my mom came out with her blue apron on and stood there with her hands on her hips as a person sometimes does when she is angry about something and is trying to decide what to do about it.

I wished—how I wished—I could have heard what they were saying about me, but I couldn't. Maybe Miss Lilly had told my parents about the lamb at school or maybe something else I'd done, which I couldn't think of, and I began to imagine all kinds of things about to happen to me.

I was down on my knees there on the alfalfa, looking through the crack and listening to pigeons cooing high in the rafters somewhere and feeling very worried. Maybe you wouldn't be interested in knowing what I did then, but I said a few words to my best Friend, whom I was beginning to like very much because He was with me all the time and always let me know when I had done right or wrong. I knew that *He* knew I hadn't done anything actually wrong on purpose, and I also knew He would understand a boy's mind.

All of a sudden, while I was still peeping

through the crack in the barn and looking at the round sun, which was going down like a big red globe, I remembered the globe on Miss Lilly's desk. And I could see one of her pretty white hands on the top of the world and the other white hand on the top of the lamb's head.

I remembered what she'd said too, and, hardly knowing it, I said out loud to myself, "Behold the Lamb of God that takes away Bill Collins's sins."

Quick as a flash, I was standing up again and starting to throw down more hay. And then I heard my mom's cheerful voice calling me to supper.

There is something wonderful about the way a boy's mom's voice sounds when it comes waving across the barnyard to tell you supper is ready. You begin to smell raw-fried potatoes right away, and you can even see the table before you get there. You can see your plate set with the silverware placed just right and your big blue mug filled with rich cold milk standing in its place. And there would be steaming, wonderful-smelling potatoes, bread and butter, a salad of some kind, and maybe a piece of cold leftover blackberry pie.

That is, you feel that way if everything is all right between you and your parents.

When I got down out of the haymow, I saw Old Man Paddler standing by our front gate, and Miss Lilly's car was there. She waved at me, and I tipped my straw hat to her, and even Old

Man Paddler turned around and said, "Hello, Bill."

Then he climbed into her car, and they drove off down the road. A jiffy later—when I was in our bathroom washing the day's different kinds of dirt off my hands and face and neck and ears—I heard the boards rumbling on the Sugar Creek bridge, and I knew it was Miss Lilly's car with Old Man Paddler in it going toward Tom and Bob Till's house, and I wondered why.

Pretty soon our family was sitting down at the table with Charlotte Ann in her high chair between Mom and me, and Dad straight across the table from us.

Supper smelled so good that I was about to forget what I was worried about, until Dad's prayer asking the blessing started me feeling bothered again. He said in his big voice, which had a sad note in it, "Please, heavenly Father, bless the boys of the Sugar Creek Gang and keep them from all harm and danger. Bless our own son with his many temptations and problems and . . ."

The second he said problems, my thoughts were back in the schoolhouse, thinking of Mr. Brown's sheep and his lumber bill and how many pounds of wool his many sheep had, of Poetry's lamb and of how it acted when it was in school, of the key to the woodshed door, which I'd given Poetry, of Miss Lilly and Old Man Paddler, and everything else.

My thoughts came back to Dad's prayer just

as he finished. "And help Mother and me to be the right kind of parents, so we shall be able to stand unashamed before Thee at Thy coming again. For Jesus' sake. Amen."

Hmm, things must have been happening fast around Sugar Creek, I thought. Something unusual was going on.

When we were half through eating, there was another car at our front gate, and this time it was Mr. Foote, Little Jim's dad. He came hurrying across the yard, looking excited about something, and the first thing I knew he was at the door.

Right away I thought of Bob Till, who had been paroled to him, or was supposed to have been. And I thought of the crazy note written in indelible pencil that Little Jim had found on the floor of his dad's car.

We finished supper right away, and I went out to where Little Jim was standing in our big swing under the walnut tree, pumping up and down, while Mom and Dad and Mr. Foote talked to each other about something—what, I didn't know.

But I did know that Mr. Foote was the township trustee, and that sometimes when boys made trouble in school the teacher had to send them to him to get a good talking to.

Things looked bad, and I was worried.

"Hi, Little Jim," I said sadly.

"What are you so sad about?" he asked, pumping himself higher.

"Nothing," I said. "Does your dad know about the lamb at school?"

Little Jim stopped pumping and said, "I'm going to stay at your house tonight."

"Why?"

"'Cause my parents are going away somewhere."

"Why?" I said, and then I remembered that Little Jim hadn't answered my other question, so I asked it again. "Does your dad know about my—about the lamb at school?"

He looked kind of sad himself at my questions, and he said, "I don't know—I don't guess so."

Just that minute Charlotte Ann started to cry about something in the house, and Little Jim lifted his feet, his small hands holding onto the rope on each side of the swing, and then he let himself sit down on the board seat—*kerplop*. "What's *that?*"

"Oh, *that!*" I said. "That's Charlotte Ann crying."

"I wish I had a little baby sister," he said wistfully.

Little Jim and I went over to his car then, and he showed me the very spot on the back floor where he'd found the note that had been written in indelible pencil.

"Where's Bob Till now?" I asked.

"Nobody knows," Little Jim said and looked sad. "He's run away again, and now if he gets arrested, he'll have to go to reform school from one to ten years, Father says."

Little Jim always called his dad "Father," which is a very respectful name, although it didn't mean he liked him any better than I did my dad, even though I called mine by a shorter name.

Dad was not only my dad, but he was my pal also. I not only obeyed him, but I also played games with him, such as checkers or caroms in the wintertime and baseball in the summer. And when we worked together, we made a game of it and had lots of fun, making the hard work seem like play.

Pretty soon, Mr. Foote came out and drove away.

Little Jim and I carried his suitcase into our house and up to my room. Then we helped Dad finish the chores and later went up to bed, neither of us knowing what important things were going to happen during the night.

10

One of the important things that happened that night was about the grandest thing that could ever have happened to Little Jim. His being the littlest member of our gang had always bothered him and made him feel as if he wasn't very important.

Just after he and I had crawled into my big bed with the clean, fresh-smelling sheets on it, my dad's steps started coming up the stairs. Dad nearly always did that—had been doing it ever since I was little. He'd come up to say good night and tell me a short story, or read me one, or quote a poem or a hymn.

When I was even littler than little, Mom taught me to say my prayer at night and tucked me in, but Dad nearly always liked to have a final look at me to see if I was all right, to see if I had any scratches or bruises or sore toes or black eyes or anything that might need attention of some kind.

Well, Dad's heavy-soled leather shoes always sounded good coming up, so Little Jim and I lay there listening and waiting in the dark, each one of us having said his prayers quietly on his knees beside the bed.

I couldn't even see Dad at first, because my eyes were still used to the light. When he cleared his throat, he was so close to us he sounded sort of like a bear growling. *Grrrrr! Garumph!*

"Any bumps?" he asked.

"Nope!" I said.

"Any scratches needing Merthiolate?"

"Nope," I said into my pillow.

"Any cuts or bruises or black eyes or smashed noses or bee stings or wood ticks that need to be pulled off? Or dirty feet that need washing or—"

Little Jim's giggle interrupted him, and Dad said to him, "Little Jim, we're proud to have you for Bill's friend. You boys want to hear a poem or something?"

With that, he started to quote what was one of my favorite poems. It was a hymn in our hymnbook and had been written—the music, I mean—by Mr. Sankey, a singer who used to travel with an evangelist named Dwight L. Moody. The poem in Dad's gruff kind of dramatic voice went like this:

"There were ninety and nine that safely lay
    In the shelter of the fold,
But one was out on the hills away,
    Far off from the gates of gold;
Away on the mountains wild and bare,
    Away from the tender Shepherd's care.

Lord, Thou hast here Thy ninety and nine—
    Are they not enough for Thee?
But the Shepherd made answer: 'This of Mine
    Has wandered away from Me . . .'"

On and on my dad's voice went, and I went out on the wings of his voice and looked all around through the mountains and hills and in the desert and among the thorns to help find the one lost sheep, which finally the Shepherd found. I even climbed up on the shoulders of the Good Shepherd and rode along with the little found sheep, only I guess maybe I was the sheep myself.

It was a great poem, and Dad finished it grandly, standing there in the dark with one hand on the post of the bedstead.

All of a sudden, Little Jim piped up like a small frog and asked—his small voice close to my right ear—"Is Jesus the Good Shepherd as well as the Lamb of God?"

And Dad said, "Yes."

When morning came and we were on our way to school, Little Jim having his lunch packed with mine, he was the happiest little guy you ever saw, because the night before, while he was at our house, Little Jim got a brand-new baby sister. He could go to the hospital to see her and his mother that very day after school.

"What's her name?" Dragonfly wanted to know right away, just as he does whenever any of the gang gets a new sister or brother. We were at the tall iron pump not far from the schoolhouse door when Dragonfly asked the question.

Little Jim knew the answer, because my mom had already been to see the baby. So he said proudly, "Her name is Jill Nadene."

Dragonfly frowned and said, trying to be funny, "I'll bet she's only about a Foote long."

And Poetry, whose parents had also already been to see the baby, came puffing up just then and said,

> "Little Jim and Jill went up the hill
>   To fetch a pail of water;
> Jim fell down and broke his crown,
>   And Jill came tumbling after."

"It's a pretty name," I said to Little Jim, remembering what he'd said last year when *my* little sister was born and I'd told him her name was Charlotte Ann.

"Sure it is!" Little Jim said.

I looked at him standing straight beside the sugar tree, and he actually looked as if he had grown several inches during the night, just like a stalk of corn when it's had a good rain. Little Jim's having a baby sister to protect was like a good rain to make him grow. He looked bigger. He felt bigger, which a boy does at a time like that.

He, Dragonfly, Poetry, and I all went inside the school then to see that the dust was all off the seats, the windows were open, and the blackboard was clean—which it wasn't very long, because Poetry and Little Jim started playing tic-tac-toe on it. Dragonfly went back to his new hobby, which was looking up words in the dictionary.

Seeing Dragonfly standing there, I said to him, "Look up the word *superstitious,* will you?"

He did. The dictionary said, "Disposed to believe in superstitions," which didn't make much sense to our minds, but whatever it was it wasn't a compliment to be that. And Dragonfly was it.

In a little while, others of the seventeen children started to come, and soon we were all in our seats again with Miss Lilly standing in her nice dress with the lily designs on it, looking out over the room at us, smiling but also looking sober.

We came to order, and then she said, "Boys and girls of District Number Nine"—which is the number of our school district in Sugar Creek Township—"I have a serious problem to present to you. As you know, Mr. Foote, our township trustee, has been instrumental in securing the release of—" Miss Lilly's blue eyes roved the room for a minute and focused on Little Tom Till, then hurried on to me and the rest of us "—the release from boys' jail of Robert Till. Robert came home Saturday afternoon and then as suddenly disappeared again. That means, of course, that he has done what is called 'jumped parole,' or violated his parole. That means plenty of trouble for him—at least a longer sentence for him in reform school.

"Now . . ." Miss Lilly looked so pretty standing there beside her desk that I got to thinking about spiders again and wished I could kill one for her. "Now," she said, "what Mr. Paddler and

80

I are trying to do is to give him still another chance, and we need your cooperation. Robert is afraid to come home and live here now, because he says everybody will make fun of him and have nothing to do with him. I have here a paper which I'd like you all to sign, and as soon as we find Robert, we'll let him read it. Perhaps he will come back to school again and continue his education. All boys need an education—almost *have* to have it these days."

Pretty soon Miss Lilly's nice speech was finished, and she read us the paper. It said:

> We, the undersigned members of District No. 9, Sugar Creek Township, want Robert Till to have another chance. We pledge ourselves not to make fun of him or at anytime say anything to make him feel humiliated. We will treat him like one of the rest of us, if he will come back to school.

Miss Lilly walked straight across to Big Jim on the other side of the room to ask him to sign first.

Big Jim didn't bat an eye. He just sat there staring at the paper lying on his desk and at Miss Lilly's gold pen, which she was holding out for him to sign with. Big Jim's hands were under his desk with his fists doubled up. I'd seen those same doubled-up fists before in the Battle of Bumblebee Hill when both of them had gone *kerwhack, wham* against Bob Till's jaw, paying Big Bob back blow for blow, fighting in self-defense and also fighting what is called an offensive battle, which my dad says is the best defense.

I'd seen those same Big Jim fists after he had split open his knuckles on a bank robber's jaw. Also, in Chicago, I'd seen his arm stretched out with a hollow needle in one of the veins. Then I'd seen the red blood of Big Jim flowing out to save Big Bob Till's life by giving a transfusion.

Now as I looked, I saw the muscles on Big Jim's jaw working. I knew he knew Bob was his worst enemy and that Bob hated him like poison and would do anything—any low-down trick—to get the best of him. And Big Jim was supposed to sign that paper?

Big Jim still just sat there, staring at the paper and not taking the pen Miss Lilly was holding out to him. I tell you, his face looked grim, and his lips were pressed firmly together. I knew he liked Miss Lilly and would maybe do anything in the world to please her if he could, but—well, what *was* he going to do? Sign or not?

Then Big Jim looked at me, and his steel-blue eyes were set and hard and also kind of sad. He looked around the room and then back again to the paper, and I thought he had made up his mind to sign. If he did, all the rest of us would.

Then just as quick as a chipmunk along Sugar Creek can make an almost invisible movement when he picks up a nut or something else to eat, Big Jim's writing hand reached out for the pen.

I sighed with relief, because I felt sorry for Bob Till in spite of his meanness and his swearing, foul-mouthed dad. I felt especially sorry for his sad-faced mother, who had never had a chance to be happy and never would have unless things were changed—or unless she let the One who had made her come into her life and make her happy inside, as my mom once told me.

But wait! Big Jim wasn't signing that paper!

He had the pen in his hand all right, then in both hands, and then, with his eyes still staring at the paper or else at his desk in front of him, he took the cap off the end of the pen and slowly pushed it onto the other end, where the pen point was. Looking up at Miss Lilly with his face set, he said, "I'm sorry, Miss Lilly. The Sugar Creek Gang can't sign that paper. We'd like to, but we can't!"

He made a quick gesture with the closed pen and handed it back to her.

11

"The Sugar Creek Gang can't sign that paper!" That's what my unbelieving ears had heard Big Jim, our leader, say.

The atmosphere in that room was thick as smoke for a while, until Miss Lilly sort of came to herself, probably feeling as if Big Jim had struck her. She stood in front of his desk with the pen in her hand and with a hurt expression on her face. Then she turned to the rest of us, a little like a fish that was out of the water, gasping for air, and as though she wanted us to sympathize with her or something.

She picked up the paper from Big Jim's desk and went up and laid it on her own. To all of us, she said in a friendly voice, "Let us all be thankful that we live in America, a country where men and women and boys and girls can be free to follow the dictates of their own consciences, without being compelled by some dictator."

Then she smiled in every direction, even in Big Jim's, and announced, "Will the first grade reading class please pass?"

And all the little girls in the small front seats scrambled from different directions and went up to the front bench, which is called a "recitation" bench, and the rest of us got busy on our own work.

My very first arithmetic problem was about a grocer who was counting the money in his cash register, and I couldn't help but think of Bob Till again. That was the reason he was in trouble in the first place—he had broken into Mr. Simondson's store and taken some money out of the cash register. And Big Jim had seen him break in through a back door in an alley.

Anyway, Miss Lilly didn't say anything more about the paper, and we didn't either, although at recess time I noticed that, when she started to pump herself a drink at the long-handled iron pump, Big Jim ran lickety-sizzle across the schoolyard and offered to pump the water for her.

She let him do it and said, "Thank you, Jim." She also smiled at him.

That day passed, and the next, and the next, but nobody saw Bob Till, and nobody said anything to us about him. He had just dropped out of sight as if a hole had opened in the earth and he had fallen in and disappeared.

Then came Friday night, when Dragonfly saw the ghost, which we saw too.

It had been a simple matter to convince our parents to let us sleep in the cave. Of course, some of our dads had gone down to look at it and to go inside and see how dry it was and that it had safe walls and a safe ceiling that wouldn't cave in.

I had my outdoor sleeping bag and my nightclothes all ready, because even though we were going to sleep in a cave, I had to wear pajamas. I walked into our living room after supper and took a look at Charlotte Ann, who was asleep in her crib. She had one cute little fist doubled up and pressed against her nose and the other was down under the blankets somewhere. She was lying on her side, breathing noisily and fast the way babies do when they're asleep.

"Well, little sister," I said, "you're still too small to know what it is to be a man and sleep out in the wild." Then I turned around and looked toward our kitchen to say good-bye to Mom.

She turned away quick with a funny smile on her face and a small chuckle.

"'S'matter?" I asked. "What's so funny?"

"Everything's fine, Billy-boy." She picked up a chair and moved it over against the kitchen wall, then straightened a curtain, and finally went to the sink, turned on a faucet, and got herself a drink.

At the kitchen door I stopped, turned around, and said, "Well . . ?"

Mom didn't say anything but set the glass she had been drinking out of in its place.

"Well," I said, wondering why she didn't say anything. "I'm going away for the night."

"What time will you want breakfast?" she asked. "Or will you boys eat at the cave?"

She didn't seem to realize how important it was for me to sleep away from home in a dangerous cave, just like a wild man, so I said, "Oh, maybe about half past seven."

"We'll have it at seven as usual," Mom said and went on working.

Outdoors, I called to Dad, who was at the barn, and said, "Good night, Dad. I'm going now."

He looked up. In his hand was a pail of mixed skim milk and bran, which he had been pouring into a long trough where about seventeen pigs were trying to eat out of a trough only long enough for twelve.

"So long, Bill," he hollered to me and turned to his work.

"So long," I called back.

Just that minute Dragonfly came whizzing up to our gate on his bicycle, and also just that minute Dad said, "I'll leave the back door open, Bill, in case for any reason you decide you'd rather sleep the rest of the night in your own warm, safe bed."

That made me angry. Imagine my dad thinking I'd be *scared* of anything, or couldn't rough it, or wouldn't be safe in an innocent cave!

"Hello, Dragonfly," I said. "Ready?"

"Mom won't let me."

"Won't let you what?" I asked.

"Mom won't let me sleep in the cave."

"I thought you said your dad said you *could.*"

And Dragonfly said, "I have *two* parents, and Mom says the cave is too close to the cemetery."

"Too close to a place where there are a lot of dead people?" It was disgusting to hear talk like that. "You're too superstitious," I said. "That's what you get for studying the dictionary so much. You know there isn't any such thing as a ghost, and—"

"You know it, and I know it, but my *mother* doesn't know it," Dragonfly said, the same thing he was always saying. "There was a great big black cat ran right across the road in front of me less than six minutes ago," he finished.

"He probably *ran* because he was afraid of you," I said, kidding him.

"But doesn't that mean bad luck?"

"Only to people who are dumb enough to believe it," I told him.

Well, the cave was on the way to Dragonfly's house, as was the old abandoned cemetery, so I rode to his house on the handlebars of his bike to help him convince the other side of his parents that it was perfectly safe for a strong boy to sleep in an innocent cave.

When we got to Dragonfly's house, his mom was as worried as anything. "You boys aren't really going to try to sleep in that old cave, are you?" she asked, and I looked at her worried face.

"Certainly," I said politely, "and I've come to ask special permission for Dragonfly. We need him. He's almost the most important member of the gang. Besides," I said, "there isn't any such thing as a ghost—Old Man Paddler says so."

Dragonfly's mom was just taking a pie out of the oven. She set it on a breadboard on the table and said slowly, "Well, I suppose I'll have to let him go. Would you like a piece of blueberry pie?"

And that settled that. We ate the pie. It also settled something else in my mind, because when we got through eating that blueberry pie, Dragonfly's teeth looked as if they had indelible pencil stains on them.

Pretty soon Dragonfly's mom had a blanket ready for him, and we rode away.

At the end of their lane, all of a sudden a big black cat darted out from behind a hedge and tried to dash across the road in front of us. Dragonfly and I were both on the bike, and the cat and both of us got tangled up. Dragonfly stepped on the brakes quick, skidded the back tire, and we both turned upside down in the ditch, on top of each other and the bicycle and also the cat, which hissed at us and beat it in some direction or other.

"What did I tell you?" Dragonfly cried from under me somewhere.

I answered from somewhere over him and the bicycle, "It wasn't the cat's fault. It's only people that believe in superstitious things that have accidents like this and get banged up."

"Do *you* believe in them?" Dragonfly asked, which was a sarcastic question.

The bicycle was still all right, so we got up and rode on. We left the bike not far from the cave and got there ahead of some of the gang. Big Jim and Circus were already there, arranging things and driving a stick or two into cracks in the wall for us to hang our clothes on.

It wasn't quite dark, but there were several hundred dozen mosquitoes around, which would want to eat us up if they could, so we gathered firewood. After a while, we'd have a fire to help keep the mosquitoes away.

In a short while, Little Jim and Poetry came along. Tom Till couldn't come, because his parents would not let him. We all sat around the mouth of the cave and talked and looked into the fire, which we had built against a rock not far from the entrance.

Time flew past, and soon it was nine o'clock and time to go to bed. We sat around inside the cave, with the two candles lit, one on a shelf on one side and one on the other, and the firelight making us feel sure no wild animal out there would dare try to get in.

Big Jim took out his New Testament and read to us a fine chapter from the book of John. The story was about a fire that the Lord Himself had built on the shore of Lake Galilee one morning, and how the Lord and Peter had a talk about how much Peter loved Him. I felt myself wishing I had been Peter and had loved the Lord as much as he did. I even wished maybe sometime I'd get to see Jesus just the way He looked when He was here on earth.

After that, each one said his own prayers, most of us saying them quietly, and then we were ready to go to sleep.

We drew straws to see who got to blow the

candles out, and Poetry and I got the job, which we did in two breaths at the same time just as we'd done before.

Then we lay down, and at once Dragonfly was squirming and saying, "Ouch! What in the world?"

"'S'matter?" most of us whispered and told him to keep still.

"I'm lying on something hard. I can feel it through my blanket."

I turned on my flashlight, and he dug down under him and pulled something out, and—would you believe it?—it was a cuff link like Old Man Paddler used in his shirts. Imagine, a cuff link in a cave!

"How'd *that* get here?" he asked.

By that time we were all sitting up and blinking our eyes and looking at the cuff link and at each other.

"Aw, that's nothing to get worried about," Poetry said sleepily, but he nudged me and put his forefinger up to his lips, which meant "Ssh!" "It might have gotten tangled up in some of our clothes, and we brought it from home. Let's go to sleep."

With that remark and explanation, which seemed to satisfy all of us, Poetry turned back to his sleeping bag.

I snapped off my flashlight, and we all were trying to sleep again. Just as I was about to doze off, and after everybody else seemed asleep, I felt Poetry nudge me gently and whisper close to my ear, *"Psst*, Bill. Are you awake?"

I was, but I didn't want to be, I was so sleepy.

"'S'matter?" I asked.

And he whispered, "Feel this." He shoved something into my hand.

I could feel right away what it was. It was a little bottle with a nipple on it, like the kind Charlotte Anne used to use, and was what Poetry had used to get his lamb to follow him to school that Monday morning.

What in the world? I thought but got my thoughts interrupted when Poetry whispered to me, "There's a ghost tied out there in the bushes waiting for you and me to go and get it."

12

I still didn't want to wake up, but Poetry was already fumbling himself out of his blanket and crawling toward the cave's exit. So I did the same thing, and the next I knew we were both far enough outside not to be heard by anybody. I wasn't interested in being mischievous at that time of night, but Poetry had everything all planned to half scare the daylights out of the gang, so I had to listen to him.

As soon as we were far enough away, we turned on our flashlights, and right away we found the lamb. It was tied to a small tree not far from the cave. Poetry had a sheet under his arm, which I hadn't noticed before, and he started to wrap it around the lamb.

By that time I was wide awake and ready for the fun, although his idea still wasn't clear to me. "What are you going to do? How are you going to make a ghost out of an innocent lamb?"

"Easy," he whispered, already working to get the nose of the lamb through the hole he'd made for it. "Now," Poetry puffed, looking something like a ghost himself in his flapping pajamas. "We'll tie you, Jerry-boy," he said in a friendly voice to the lamb, "right behind the sycamore, and the rest will be easy."

Well, it *was* easy. We tied the ridiculous-looking lamb to the sycamore tree and crawled back slowly to the cave. At the entrance, we stopped and listened and didn't hear anything. For a second Poetry turned his flashlight on the lamb.

I almost jumped out of my green pajamas, the way that lamb looked with its big eyes staring into the light, its absolutely grotesque white clothes, its eyeholes and its nose hole and long white tail, and also the white horns Poetry had made for it.

I don't know what Poetry's plan was for after that, for just that second his innocent lamb let out a mournful bleat, and then another and another, and tried to get loose from itself.

Behind us in the cave we heard noises, the rest of the gang waking up and talking. I saw flashlights going on, and the fun had started.

Poetry and I darted behind some bushes and turned our flashlights on the crazy-acting lamb.

We also watched the gang come crawling and tumbling out of the cave. They certainly looked ridiculous themselves. Big Jim with his purple pajamas on, Little Jim with his half-a-dozen-colored ones, Circus with white pajamas that were so short they came halfway to his knees and almost to his elbows. Dragonfly's were striped, the stripes running around instead of up and down. And most of them were rubbing their eyes and looking at the lamb as if they were seeing a ghost.

I tell you there was plenty of excitement around there for a few minutes.

As soon as the gang found out it was a trick, they were all set to take Poetry and me down to Sugar Creek and duck us, pajamas and all, but the lamb interrupted their plans. With all that noise, it got terribly scared. It bleated pitifully and was so afraid that Big Jim took things in his own hands and said, "That lamb has got to go home to its mother."

Then he said, "Get your pants and shoes on, all of you, and follow me—*all* of you!" he finished his command sternly.

Well, Poetry took off the lamb's ridiculous suit, and it didn't take long for us to get ready to take the lamb home. Big Jim made us do it, saying the little thing would probably be scared half to death if we didn't.

Pretty soon we were all walking along toward Poetry's pasture, where there would be other lambs and sheep. As you know, Poetry lived closer to the old sycamore tree than any of the rest of us.

I followed right behind Big Jim, holding my flashlight for him to see and noticing the lamb as he carried it on his shoulder the way a farmer does who knows how to carry a lamb. And all the time, I was thinking about the "Ninety and Nine" and looking at the lamb. As we trudged along, I reached out my hand once and put it on the lamb's withers, and the poor little thing was trembling as though it was cold and terribly afraid.

I could see Poetry was sorry, for he had a very tender heart for animals and wouldn't hurt one for anything, that being one reason he had been able to make the lamb a pet in the first place.

It was when we were on our way *back* to the cave that the thing happened. We knew it was nearer to go past Bumblebee Hill to get to the cave than any other way. So we decided to go that way, even though the old cemetery was at the top.

It was still not later than ten o'clock, but it was chilly for that time of night, and the dew was on the grass, making us glad we all had our pajamas covered, or they'd have been wet at the cuffs and we'd have had to sleep with them that way later on. For a minute I remembered Dad's words about coming home and sleeping in my own nice, warm bed if I wanted to, but I wouldn't have done it for the world.

We came to Bumblebee Hill and started to go across it. We were about halfway, right close to the place where I'd once smashed Little Tom's nose in the fight we'd had there, when all of a sudden, Dragonfly stopped dead still and said, *"Psst!* Listen," which we all did, some of us bumping into the ones in front of us who had stopped quicker than we had.

"See!" Dragonfly hissed. "There goes that *lamb*, running toward the cemetery."

We looked up, and that's exactly what it did look like, away up there at the top of the hill.

"How in the world—" Poetry said.

We had opened the gate at Poetry's farm and put the lamb inside, yet here it was out and running, not toward us but in a different direction.

Well, we gave chase. We all started to run toward the top. We tried to turn our flashlights on it, but it had already disappeared through the fence. In a half minute, the six of us were at the top of the hill, going through the fence right at the place where Old Man Paddler had torn his shirt the Sunday before.

It was Dragonfly who stopped us. "Wait!" he cried, when the rest of us had gone through.

I turned around, and there he was, in his prison pajamas, standing on the other side. "I-I-I'm scared! There might be a *real* ghost! Hey! *Hey!* There *is* one! *Look!*" he shouted in a scream that was smothered in fear.

We looked in every direction and finally saw something white streaking out across the cemetery, past Old Man Paddler's wife's grave, moaning and running or flying or something. Then it started beating it toward Sugar Creek and the cave.

That settled that! That wasn't any innocent lamb! It was an honest-to-goodness ghost, of which there weren't any.

"After him!" Big Jim ordered.

And we *were* after him—even Dragonfly, getting up a little bravery from the rest of us. Being brave is contagious, you know. You follow the leader if *he* is brave, and you aren't scared unless *he* is, which Big Jim wasn't. Or else you can be scared and brave at the same time, which is the way I felt.

Lickety-sizzle, dodge, plunge, rush, hurry, dash, fall-down-get-up-quick, plunge on—that's the way we tore through the woods after that white ghost. Our minds were made up to catch whatever it was.

"Look!" Dragonfly puffed again from somewhere among us. "It's headed straight for the cave!"

My flashlight showed the cave right ahead of us. The ghost or whatever it was—we didn't know—stumbled over a log and down it went *kerplop* right in front of the entrance.

Big Jim, who was in the lead, with Circus right behind him and me next, got there almost at the same time. Big Jim made a head-first tackle as he does in a football game, and then he and the ghost were on the ground together, scrambling and wrestling.

The ghost was panting and fighting like everything, and then all of a sudden it worked itself loose from Big Jim. There was a ripping and tearing sound as Big Jim held onto some of its clothes, and the next thing we knew, the ghost was gone, and Big Jim stood there, holding in his hands a big white torn shirt.

"It went inside the cave!" Dragonfly whispered.

Well, I tell you, we were excited. Nothing like this had ever happened before. It couldn't be so, I thought. I was merely having a crazy dream because I was trying to sleep in a cave.

And yet it wasn't a dream, because right there in front of my eyes was a torn white shirt in Big Jim's hands, and—

All of a sudden Poetry said, "There's your other cuff link, Dragonfly—in the cuff of that shirt."

I knew *ghosts* didn't wear shirts with gold cuff links in them.

While we were all gathering around Big Jim and also watching the cave to see that no ghost came out, I noticed something else about the shirt. I gasped out loud. There, as plain as day, right on the back of the white shirt, was a crooked bit of needlework in the exact spot where my Mom had sewed up the white shirt belonging to Old Man Paddler himself only a few days ago.

What in the world! I thought again. *Why— why, that's Old Man Paddler's shirt!*

And that could mean only one thing. The ghost was Old Man Paddler himself.

"That's Old Man Paddler's shirt!" I exclaimed. "See there, Poetry! That's the same shirt he tore on the barbed wire fence at the graveyard last Sunday afternoon!"

"Old Man Paddler can't run that fast!" Big Jim said grimly.

We all knew that was right. The old man couldn't run at all—unless maybe he could if he was terribly scared. Yet, whoever it was couldn't have been a ghost, since ghosts didn't wear shirts with cuff links or stumble over fallen logs. In fact, if it had been a real ghost, a log wouldn't even have been in its way. It could go through a log like a radio wave goes through a house and is still a radio wave on the other side.

Just then Poetry gasped and said, "Look, everybody! There's a pencil clipped into the pocket of the shirt—an indelible pencil!"

And there was.

Well, we had to do something. We couldn't just stand around at a time like that. We decided to go inside the cave. Maybe. If we weren't too scared.

Big Jim asked, "Anybody want to go home?" He looked around at Dragonfly and all of us.

And Dragonfly said with a stutter, "I-I want to, but I w-w-won't!"

And I say we *all* wanted to but wouldn't.

"All right, everybody!" Big Jim gave the word. "When he comes out, *grab* him! And look out for smashed noses!"

I couldn't believe it. We were going to go right into the enemy's mouth. *We were going to go inside that cave!*

13

First Big Jim hollered into the cave, and his voice sounded very fierce. "Come out of there, whoever you are! We'll give you until we count ten, and then we're coming in!"

All we heard in reply was a weird echo, which came floating back like a screech owl's voice across the hills. *"Count ten,"* the echo said.

We all had left most of our clothes in that cave, and some of us had watches and knives and other things of value there, so we had to go in. And I certainly wasn't going to go home and go in our unlocked back door and sleep in any old nice, warm, safe bed.

Then Big Jim started to count, very loud: *"One, two, three, four, five, six, seven, eight, nine, TEN!"*

We waited, and no ghost came out, and there wasn't any answer.

So Big Jim gave the order: "Follow Circus and me!" With that, he and Circus, with two flashlights making a white path for them, stooped low, shot the lights inside, and looked in, while the rest of us waited, all holding our breath and also holding some sticks and clubs, which we'd found close by.

"It's empty." Big Jim turned to us, and so did Circus.

In we all went, and, sure enough, there wasn't a thing inside except the rock walls, and our sleeping bags and clothes and things, and the two lonely candles looking like a couple of stalagmites standing on their shelves, with no stalactites reaching down from above.

And now what to do! The ghost or whoever or whatever was gone, so we either had to give up and go to sleep or just go to sleep. We looked funny and felt crazy and scared and disappointed. If we hadn't had the shirt, maybe we wouldn't have believed it, but we *had* the shirt, and it was absolutely Old Man Paddler's.

Big Jim called us to order then and said, "I may as well tell you, to relieve your minds, that it wasn't a ghost!"

"It was too," I said. "It went in this cave, didn't it?"

"Anybody see it come in here except Dragonfly?" Circus asked.

"I did," I said, "with my own eyes—I think."

"Well, it isn't here now. Anybody know who it was?" Big Jim said again. "If not, we'll let it go and get some sleep."

"I s-saw it come in here headfirst," Dragonfly said fiercely. "I knew there was going to be a ghost because a black cat—"

"Order!" Big Jim demanded again, and there was.

"Listen! What was *that!*" Dragonfly exclaimed.

We'd all heard it. It was the sound of somebody coming!

As plain as day and even plainer, we heard

footsteps coming toward us from somewhere. It sounded as if something was coming from behind the cave walls, or else something was already inside and walking around unseen right among us—or maybe even walking on the ceiling upside down. If it *was* a ghost, or if there was any such thing as a ghost, it could do that.

I looked at Big Jim, and I saw for the first time that *he* was afraid, so I let myself be afraid too, without being ashamed of it.

Nearer and nearer, louder and louder came those footsteps—from somewhere behind the walls?—and then they stopped, so close beside me and behind me and in front of me, that I thought I could have reached out and touched whoever or whatever it was. I wished I'd hurry and wake up, because this was the craziest dream I'd ever had.

And then all of a sudden, there in front of us, crawling into the mouth of the cave, was an old man with white hair and long white whiskers. He had a cane and a yardstick in one hand and a long flashlight in the other, and it was Old Man Paddler himself.

It couldn't be, and yet it was.

"Good evening, everybody! May I come into your house?"

The minute I heard his voice, I knew it was actually him and that I wasn't in a dream.

"I'm sorry to disturb your night's rest this way, but it's a long way home around the old wagon trail, so I decided to take a shortcut. I guess I'd better rest a bit first. I'm pretty tired.

Had a little business to do in town, stopped a while in the old cemetery there at my wife's grave. I guess I must have gone to sleep there. Anyway, something woke me up."

While he was talking and his whiskers were bobbing up and down in the light of the candles, which we'd already lit, I was looking at his gray shirt, which he certainly had on, and I knew the ghost hadn't been Old Man Paddler.

He shivered then and said, "It's cold in here. Ah . . ." He stopped, and I could see from his eyes that he had an idea and was going to spring it on us.

"Listen," he said, "I've something very important to talk to you boys about. If you'll gather up your sleeping bags and clothes and follow me . . ."

With that, he sidled over to a corner of the cave where there was a rocky ledge and gave it a little push. And, *wow!* The rock moved! And there, as plain as candlelight could make it, was a hole leading back into the hill somewhere.

"What's *that?*" different ones of us cried in absolute astonishment.

The old man turned around to us. "There used to be a little underground stream coming through here and flowing out into Sugar Creek. The other end, I just discovered this week, is in my own cellar. Follow me, and I'll show you. Bring your stuff along, and you can sleep in my cabin. I'll make you some sassafras tea to warm you up a bit. You're all shivering with the cold," he finished, which we were.

Well, things were beginning to make sense—all except that white torn shirt.

Suddenly Big Jim said, "Look, Mr. Paddler! Is this your shirt?" He held out the shirt, all torn to shreds, toward the old man.

Mr. Paddler started as if somebody had stuck him with a pin. "Where did you get *that*?"

"I just tore it off Bob Till ten minutes ago," Big Jim said, and that made *me* start and all the rest of us also.

For a minute there was silence, that is, until we heard a door slam faraway somewhere. Poetry looked at me quick and I at him, and all of a sudden we knew that we had known something a long time. There was a door in the cellar of Old Man Paddler's cabin at the other end of the tunnel into whose jaws we were looking right that very minute.

And that was the beginning of the end of this story, which is almost too long now, about the secret hideout inside the hill.

"Bob Till," Old Man Paddler said, "has been staying at my cabin this week, while I've been trying to make arrangements to have the law give him still another chance. I keep thinking, what if it was my William or one of my other sons, who is dead now. I think if I can teach him a few things which his father should have taught him a long time ago, we can make a decent citizen of him, and maybe he will become a Christian. A boy has to *hear* the gospel, you know, before he can be saved."

There was more that Old Man Paddler said, but that is enough for you to know right now.

Well, we gathered up our clothes, putting most of them on. Then, carrying blankets and sleeping bags, we went into that dark hole in the side of the hill. We followed Old Man Paddler back and back, winding and winding, stooping here and there, and passing little piles of dirt and rock, which he and Bob had made when they had had to dig through places that were too small for a man or boy to go through.

Pretty soon we came to a new door. And then we were in Old Man Paddler's cellar. And then we were up in his fine, neat old cabin. We'd saved ourselves a mile of walking.

"Boy, that will save him a lot of walking when he has to go to town, won't it?" Poetry said to me, puffing hard and always glad for anything that would save walking or working.

"It'll be especially good next winter," the old man said, having heard what Poetry said, and he busied himself lighting the fire in his stove to make some sassafras tea to get the shivers out of us.

At that minute, I heard somebody in Old Man Paddler's upstairs coughing a little as though he had a cold, and it sounded like a boy's cough.

"That's Bob Till," Old Man Paddler said. "I've been taking care of him. Poor fellow, he hasn't even had enough clothes of his own, so I've been letting him wear some of mine. I suppose that's where that white shirt came from.

He'd been in the cemetery doing a little cleaning up around my sons' graves. He was afraid of being seen in the daytime, so I let him go at night. He's still got a sense of shame, you know, like most boys have if you can dig deep enough to find it—or maybe if Almighty God can get a chance to put it into him."

So we slept in the cabin, and I don't need to tell you about that.

But this much you ought to know: The next Monday morning, when the seventeen pupils of the Sugar Creek School, No. 9, were all sitting in their seats studying, or supposed to be studying, all of a sudden Big Jim raised his hand.

Miss Lilly looked at him and nodded, and he motioned for her to come to his desk, which she did.

I had been trying to find out what that same Mr. Brown, who had had trouble with his wool and his sheep and his bank account and his lumber bill, was going to do about his *coal* bill, so it was easy for me to look up and watch and listen to see what was going on in Big Jim's mind.

And do you know what? He said to Miss Lilly—and his voice was very clear and like a man's—"The Sugar Creek Gang is ready now to sign that paper, if we may, please."

And so was all the rest of the school.

I really don't know whether anything as important could happen to the Sugar Creek Gang as what I've just written to you about, but if anything does happen, I'll take plenty of time to tell you about it.

In fact, I can almost feel that something *is* going to happen. That very afternoon, after school was out and I was on my way home, I had to go past Circus's house for something, and his dad's big hunting dogs, with their long noses and their long voices, had something up a tree and were making plenty of dog noise.

"Hello there, Bill Collins," Circus's dad's husky voice called to me. "Fall is almost here, and I've planned a hunting trip some dark, drizzling night, and I'd like all the Sugar Creek Gang to go along. I saw coon tracks along the mouth of the branch this morning."

I went on home, thinking about that hunting trip and hoping my parents would let me go. It would be fun to go hunting along with the gang, walking in the flickering of a lantern through the dark woods and along Sugar Creek, hearing the long-tongued bawling of the hounds.

And we might even catch—well, 'most anything.

The *Sugar Creek Gang* Series: